DOCTRINE OF AVOIDANCE

Book Three of the Red Javelin Series

ROSS HARRINGWAY

Omega Press
El Paso, Texas

DOCTRINE OF AVOIDANCE

OMEGA PRESS

An imprint of Omega Communications Group, Inc.

For information contact:

Omega Press
5823 N. Mesa, #839
El Paso, Texas 79912

FIRST EDITION

Printed in the United States of America

OTHER BOOKS BY ROSS HARRINGWAY

FROM OMEGA PRESS

The Clovis Legacy Series

The Forbidden Region
Reign of Death
Shadows in the Dark
Weakness is Provocative
Illusion of Freedom
Burdened with Morality

The Red Javelin Chronicles

Red Javelin
Shroud of Cleopatra

Editor's note: Some of the events in this novel occur simultaneously with the novels Red Javelin and Shroud of Cleopatra.

PROLOGUE

He woke up to a fervent shaking of his shoulders and an open handed slap to his face. Hal Palmer opened his eyes and gazed into the lovely face of one of his younger sisters, Diana. She was yelling his name and shaking his arms in a frantic attempt to wake him. Hal took in a desperate, deep breath as he sat upright and looked around him. He was in his dormitory room on the Newton Academy Campus. He was clothed in a white t-shirt with the Newton Academy logo across the chest and a pair of dark shorts covered his lower extremities. That was his first clue that something was amiss. When he had fallen asleep, Hal Palmer had been nude next to a lovely lady that he had made love to. The fact that he was wearing any clothing at all confused him. He reached over to the other side of his bed and found that it was empty. His one night lover had slipped away without even a goodbye.

His bed was surrounded by seven of his sisters, who were also cadets at the Academy. The seven women were looking down at him with concern in their eyes.

Hal felt as if his head was being pounded by a hammer. He was unable to focus and felt dizzy. He tried to speak, but his voice was dry.

"You missed two days of class!" exclaimed his sister Iris. "We were all worried sick about you."

"Water," Hal was finally able to say with a raspy and weak voice.

"Get him some water!" Jessie Palmer barked at the gathering of cadets and Palmer family members. She waited impatiently as the youngest Palmer sister, Courtney, fetched a cup of water from the dormitory bathroom.

Hal gratefully accepted the cup of water and drank it in one gulp. He blinked his eyes as he tried to focus on the crowd around him. He recalled meeting the very sexy and desirable woman at a bar on Friday night, just a few hours after his last class for the week. She had been wearing a skin tight, low cut silver top and a very short black mini-skirt. Hal recalled that when the woman approached him she smiled and asked him if he could buy her a drink. She told him that she was in the medical section at the Academy. After the third drink, she suggested that they go back to his dorm room and have sex. Hal immediately took her up on her offer. He recalled arriving at his room with the woman, kissing her passionately once the doors slid shut behind them. He vividly recalled feeling her curvaceous body in his hands, undressing her as quickly as he could. He still remembered the look in her eyes as he made love to her on his bed. He recalled that shortly after making love to the woman he fell asleep and remembered nothing else until he was forcefully awakened by his sister.

His seven sisters were named Diana, Iris, Helena, Jessie, Courtney, Barbara and Nova. Each of them were dressed in their fuchsia colored one piece Newton Academy cadet uniforms. All seven had different insignias on their shoulder patches that distinguished them based on their declared major at the military institution. Hal was the only one form his family that was studying to be a pilot while each of his sisters were engineering, computer or science branch students.

In addition to his seven sisters there were several medical personnel and a female Captain wearing the ominous black uniform of the Military Intelligence Branch, also known as the militzia. The woman had a shaved head to display the tattoo of a red dragon that covered the majority of her skull. She had a set of silver earrings that were in the shape of upside down crosses. She had long fingers with long, dark fingernails and seemed to be unusually slender. Hal noted that the officer had a pearl handled laser pistol attached to her utility belt that was surrounded by several knives in black sheaths.

"What happened to me?" Hal finally was able to ask. "How many classes did I miss?"

"Two days' worth," an elderly doctor dressed in a white uniform with a name tag that read "Mahmoud" responded.

"Two days?" Hal placed his hands on his foreheaad. "My head is pounding."

"What do you see when you close your eyes?" Mahmoud asked him.

Hal opened his eyes and blinked a few times as he considered the question. "I see a pattern of blue dots, all in a symmetrical design, surrounded by a black background. Why?"

Mahmoud nodded at the MI Captain, "The same as the other six victims."

"Victims?" Hal tried to stand up at the mention that he might have been the target of some criminal act. As he did so, he felt his knees give out under him and he was saved from falling flat on his face by Diana, Helena and Iris

Palmer. The three sisters pushed him back onto his bed.

"I should have warned you not to try and stand up too quickly," Mahmoud told him. He approached Hal and gave him an injection into his neck. He noticed that Hal seemed a bit startled by the fact that he injected him. "Don't worry. It is only a vitamin and steroid compound to help you regain your strength. You are going to be fine."

"I'm a victim?" Hal asked slowly, feeling the fatigue and the ache all over his body. "A victim of what? How can you tell?"

"My eyes are actually medical scanners that were implanted by my request," Mahmoud responded. "I can x-ray a patient with the blink of my eyes and scan your entire body in a few seconds. I have a microscopic computer chip in my brain that processes the data my electronic eyes take in in a few seconds. I found that your brain has been scanned by some highly advanced technology and that your DNA was stolen."

"How was my DNA stolen?"

"The perpetrator drained over a pint of your blood, cadet. Most likely the woman you slept with will be creating a few thousand duplicates of you to do her bidding."

The female in the black uniform finally joined the

conversation. She pulled one of the small stools that were in Hal's dormitory room next to his bed and looked into his eyes as she sat down. "Cadet, you were used."

Hal stared into the dark eyes of the Captain and squinted, "How was I used?"

"You brought a woman back to your dorm room Friday night. You met her at the bar that you cadets hang out at, the one called Newton Rules. Do you remember her?"

Hal nodded, "Yeah. Yes ma'am I do. She was beautiful. We met at the bar. I had never seen her around campus. I thought nothing of it since she told me she was a medical student and since I am in the astronaut program it made sense that we never crossed paths before."

The Captain shook her head from left to right, "She isn't even a student. We caught her image on the security cams at the entrance of the dormitory. We identified her as a medical doctor named Nicolette Rosenburg. She isn't even a citizen of planet New Quebec. She arrived here, how we do not know, and was able to track you down and bring you to your room and drug you. Any idea why she would do that?"

Hal shook his head at the mention of the Rosenburg name. "She said her name was Nikki Ross and that she was a med student here. Rosenburg? Is she from the same family that tried to kill me and my friends on the Blood Moon?"

"The very same family," Mahmoud nodded. "You probably had your brain scanned just like the other cadets that were targeted this weekend. That's why your head is aching and you are seeing the geometric patterns of blue dots each time you close your eyes."

"Those damn Rosenburg's," Hal hissed angrily. "Because of them a lot of my friends are dead. Please tell me that you caught her."

"Negative," the Captain responded coldly. "But you must understand Cadet Palmer that you were not the only one that was visited by Doctor Rosenburg."

"Who else?" Hal wanted to know.

"Cadet Corbin Kelso was found in his room in the same condition as you," the Captain told him. "Curious that the two most talented male cadet pilots are picked up by the same woman, at exactly the same time, in separate locations and had their memories scanned. Did you have sex with her?"

"That's rather personal," Hal responded.

"And I am investigating a possible criminal act, so answer my question or I will go to the Dean of the

Academy and have you expelled for interfering with my job. I will only ask you one more time. Did you have sex with her?"

Hal nodded, "Yes. Yes I did. Afterwards, I fell asleep. I wake up to all of you. She must have left me after I fell asleep. I didn't even hear her leave my room. I don't know what to think."

The Captain pursed her lips and stood up, "Nicolette Rosenburg did not have a twin sister, cadet. You were seduced by a duplicate. A clone. While the duo Nicolette's were seducing you and Kelso there were five men that seduced five female cadet pilots at the same time. Those five girls woke up in the same condition that you are in."

Hal felt his headache fading thanks to the inoculation given to him by Mahmoud. Hal hated the Roseburg's due to the fact that they had caused the deaths of his friends on the Blood Moon. "Was the man that went after the women a Rosenburg?"

The Captain shook her head, "No. We scanned his image and found that he was Drayton Love Easter. All five men were this Mister Easter. All five of the women were in the top ten of the astronaut program. Do you know Drayton Love Easter?"

"No," Hal responded defensively. "Should I know him?"

"He is the best friend of a man named Les Gillis from Clovis Academy. You do know him?"

"Yes, he was on the Blood Moon with me."

"And Gillis never mentioned Mister Easter?"

"Never to me."

"There were five of him and each one sought out the five girls to get them behind closed doors and scan their minds. All seven victims are cadet pilots with the best grade marks and woke up with the same symptoms. Very curious."

"Are you accusing me of anything?" Hal demanded of the Captain. "I told you that I do not know the man!"

"And I believe you," the Captain assured him. "I am not accusing you of anything. Not yet."

"Which of the other cadets were targeted?" Hal asked in an attempt to change the tenor of the questions which he felt were accusatory in nature.

"Tammie Woods, Sheila Lei, Astral Provo, Cassandra Bolton and Erica Pham. All five met the same man, at the same time, at different locations around campus and were taken behind closed doors by him. He was also a clone of the original man named Love Easter. The clones did their research. They knew exactly where all seven of you would be and when you would be there."

Hal grunted after hearing the names. All five of the women were his friends. Tammie Woods was the cousin of Torch Woods, one of Hal's friends that died on the Blood Moon. He felt his blood pressure rising due to the anger he felt. "How do you know it was a clone?"

"Because the real Drayton Love Easter is an officer serving on planet New Berlin. We have that information confirmed. He is living in another solar system and therefore it was impossible for him to be here. These were duplicates that set upon you, Hal Palmer. And I am willing to bet that your mind and memories were not all that they were after."

"What else could anyone possibly want from me? I'm just a cadet."

"They wanted your DNA, Cadet Palmer."

"Why would anyone want my DNA? Why would they want Kelso's DNA and Lei's and the others? It makes no sense."

"We believe that Doctor Nicolette Rosenburg is trying to put together an army," the Captain stood up as she spoke. "She has cloned herself and has plenty of medical help from the replicas of herself. But she had no pilots.

Now she has the DNA and memories of seven of the most talented cadet pilots on the planet. Now she can clone you and your friends, make thousands of each of you, and then she will have her corps of pilots."

Hal shook his head, "But for what purpose? Why go through all that trouble to get the DNA of a few cadets here on New Quebec?"

"Because we are in the same solar system as Sikorsky's Planet, Cadet Palmer. I believe that Nicolette Rosenburg will be making the army of cloned pilots' right here on this planet. She will unleash them when she determines that the time is right. The last questions I have for you cadet are as follows: Are you the real Hal Palmer? And if you are, do you mind if we run some tests on you?"

Hal noticed that the name tag on the Captain read "Sikorsky." He sighed, "Do I have a choice in the matter?"

"No Cadet Palmer, you do not. Follow Doctor Mahmoud and I. We have much more to discuss."

"Shit," Hal said under his breath as he stood up. Although he wanted to know what was done to him as much as anyone else did, Hal Palmer did not trust the Royal Family. Given that a Sikorsky was involved in the investigation, Hal had a feeling of dread that gave him more apprehension that the mystery that he was now a part of. He followed the Captain and was grateful that his seven sisters refused to leave his side. He had no desire to be left alone with a Sikorksy, especially one with a dragon etched into her head.

As they walked out of his dormitory room, Hal was assisted by his sisters Diana and Helena who were holding on to his right and left arms respectively. He was able to keep his balance without their help but having them there made him feel better.

"We know that you were well paid by the Rosenburg Corporation for the injuries you sustained on the Blood Moon. I trust you have invested your settlement money well?"

"I am comfortable, Captain." Hal grunted. "If you are trying to ask me my feelings about the Rosenburg's, you do not need to. I hate them all. They killed friends of mine. I was left to die on the surface of that chlorine gas covered moon. If it were not for Marco Andolini I might have bled to death. The amount that family paid me was not enough."

"You are loyal to Marco Andolini and your friends. That is good to know. So, Cadet Palmer, are you loyal to the Glorious Leader?" Captain Sikorsky inquired of him as they approached the elevator.

Hal glared at her for a moment before responding. "Of course I am, Captain. What is going on?"

The woman looked over the eight Palmer siblings and sneered at them as she answered his question. "A war is going on, cadets. Since you are all cadets you are subject to being called up to the ranks at any time. The Glorious Leader just might need each of you to defend the homeland sooner than you think. What happened here to you has been happening at Academies all over the eight solar systems. Somebody is building an army of pilots and students of tactical warfare. We believe that all of this is in preparation for a rebellion."

"Who would dare do such a thing?" Iris Palmer demanded.

"Someone that wants my dear grandfather removed from power," the Captain told her. "I know that the majority of you are in the technical and engineering courses. But you have all taken the basic weaponry proficiency courses. I hope for your sakes that you each paid attention during those courses."

"I haven't finished those courses ma'am," Courtney Palmer said.

Sikorsky smiled at her, "Courtney, right? You are what? Seventeen? That is old enough to die for your

Glorious Leader. We in the Royal Family appreciate all of your sacrifices. Just make sure that before you die, you kill as many of the enemy as you can."

Courtney swallowed hard as she heard the comments from the Captain. She looked at the oldest sisters Diana and Helena for some reassurance in their eyes. She saw none.

CHAPTER ONE

The binary star system of Sikorsky's Planet provided light and warmth for eight planets and forty lunar sized bodies. The closest planet to the largest sun was called Planet Hades due to the extreme heat and the inability to support life forms. The second planet was named Planet Rycon, an Akarzdamedian terra-formed world that was conquered by humanity two centuries ago. It was populated by over two billion humans and another half a billion Akarzdamedians. Rycon was ruled by Tania Rendon, a century and a half year old daughter of the Glorious Leader, and her offspring. Rycon was filled with blue skies, earth-like vegetation, oceans and lakes of drinkable water and fertile soil to grow crops. It was a thriving world which would attract many humans seeking opportunity.

Skilled clones sent in by Penelope Rosenburg were

able to infiltrate the capital city of planet Rycon and some of the other larger populated cities. They were men and women that were created from the DNA of Frank Garrison, Drayton Love-Easter, Ella Ragnarsson, Nicolette Rosenburg and others that had died too young on the Space Station that Penelope Rosenburg had once lived on. The clones of Ella Ragnarsson each had the memories of Penelope Rosenburg implanted in their brains so that they would be loyal to the cause of insurrection.

One of those clones called herself Penella Cuarenta y Cinco. The number, which was in Spanish, represented the order in which she had been created. She was able to use stealth to get close to the main housing complex for Tania Rendon and her family. Penella planted lethal explosives around each of the large mansions, some of them as high as twelve floors, and waited in the shadows of the large trees for Tania Rendon to return home from work. When Rendon's eight transport ships landed in the massive courtyard in the center of the mansions, Penella delayed executing her mission until she could confirm Rendon's presence. Once she did so, Penella detonated the charges she had placed.

The explosives brought the large mansions down in a hailstorm of fire, brick and metal. Tania Rendon and the majority of her family were killed instantly in the eruptions. Those that survived were crushed under the rubble. With Rycon now left without the dictatorship of Rendon, the clones of Garrison and the others began to sow the seeds of discontentment in the other cities. The inhabitants began to believe that perhaps Rycon could become a world free of the cruelty of the Royal Family. Soon there was fighting in the streets as man, woman and Akarzdamedian opted for a different path for the planet they had grown to love as their home.

The *Antony 9* had been flying through space at full speed for several days. The commander of the Super Raumschiff, Penelope Rosenburg, had one thought on her mind.

Murder.

Not the unjustified type of murder where one strangles or stabs a person without reason. Her idea of murder was fully warranted as she was at war with her own family. She was a descendant of Vladimir Sikorsky, the Glorious Leader of the eight solar systems that were under his dictatorial rule. After witnessing numerous barbaric acts committed by members of her family, she set out on a one woman mission to start a civil war. She intended to kill all of the descendants of Vladimir Sikorsky that were currently in any form of power. She was cognizant that her goal was a lofty one as there were close to a million members of that subset of humanity.

She needed help. She first recruited two of her sisters that were medical doctors and experts in the replicant sciences. With their assistance, they began collecting DNA samples and brain memories of good men and women that were being killed by the Sikorsky regime. They created an army of duplicates. They first made twenty-five clones of a man named Frank Garrison that had been a security officer serving on Space Station Cy-7. Their second masterpiece was an equal number of clones of a Clovis Academy cadet senior named Drayton Love-Easter. Both men had either been murdered by the Rosenburg family assassins.

Penelope next convinced a man of good will named Charles Bennington to join her little rebellion. He had been the chief of the Criminal Investigation Division on Space Station Cy-7 and witnessed some of the same atrocities that Rosenburg had. As the small band of rebels embarked on their mission, all of the members save Bennington submitted to brain scans and offered DNA samples for the purpose of creating more clones. The three Rosenburg sisters had collected DNA from other individuals, one was an intergalactic assassin named Ella Ragnarsson. Another was the samples they saved of their deceased brother named Cush. But the sister devised a scheme in which they would clone the physical body but download the brain of one of their own.

Penelope dispatched two dozen Raumschiffs from locations on other worlds to rendezvous with her and her sisters. She stocked those space craft with clones of her sisters, Love Easter and sent them on missions to other planets to gather more DNA from selected targets and create instability for the Sikorsky controlled governments. Many of the missions were successful and reported that thousands of pilots, tacticians and cadets had been duplicated. Penelope was pleased with their progress and hoped that her team of traitors would soon unleash their army against the delusive Glorious Leader.

As they worked diligently on creating their army of freedom fighters, they selected as their first target the Battle Cruiser Fleet under Admiral Cardenas. He was easy to recruit due to the fact that the Royal Family had caused the death of his son on the Blood Moon. He supplied them with two new Raumschiff space craft for their expanding army. They next ambushed the four science cruisers that were on the outer edge of space. They were successful in killing all of the descendants of Sikorsky on those four ships.

On their return, they sent in some of their clones to create an insurrection on planet New Berlin. Leaving those covert operatives on that human colony of almost twenty million people, they targeted their next potential allies.

They would attempt to turn the crew and commanders of the Second Fleet of Battle Cruisers that were patrolling the solar system of planet New Sao Paolo. Bennington, Tucson Garrison, Drayton Love-Easter #8, Penelope, Kristin and Nicolette Rosenburg spent hours studying the crew members. Their resumes were gone over with attention to detail.

The Second Fleet consisted of five of the best Battle Cruisers in the entire Space Command. Each ship had a crew of over one thousand five hundred. Half of them were pilots and some of them were elite pilots in either the Search and Rescue Division or the Deep Space Reconnaissance Division. If they could be convinced to join the rebellion they would make a formidable opponent for a first strike on the home planet of Vladimir Sikorsky.

"The Amistad is the flagship of the fleet." Penelope told a group of her closest confidants as they sat down around a conference table in the command section of the Raumschiff called the *Peacemaker*. Her sisters Kristen and

Nicolette were there as well as Bennington. Drayton #8 and Tucson Garrison were sitting on the far end of the table listening to her every word. "It is commanded by Captain Bruce Allen, a veteran of many battles and a great tactician."

"An Allen? I thought all of them left the service after their mandatory service time was up," Drayton #8 remarked. "Their family is more loyal to the profit motive than the service."

"True, Dray. True. But there were circumstances that occurred in the life of this specific Allen that led him to choose to stay in the service. He rose up the ranks quickly. We need him if our rebellion will succeed." Penelope snapped her fingers and the ship computer displayed a three dimensional image of Bruce Allen. "He is a good man from what we could pull from his service records. The problem will be his executive officer, chief pilot, security chief, chief medical officer, chief of explorations and several of their subordinate officers. They are all Royal Family members. We will have to eliminate them as we did the Royal's on the Science Cruisers. The Admiral on the Amistad is named Khan. From what his service records indicate he is a brilliant man and fierce warrior."

"When I was a young officer I served under Khan

when he was a Captain," Bennington informed the group. "He was well respected and I recall him to be a reasonable man."

Penelope snapped her fingers once more and the entire room became dark and the computer displayed a three dimensional replica of the binary star solar system of Sikorsky's Planet. "If we can get the Second Fleet to lock down all traffic in and out of Sikorsky's Planet then that might force the Glorious Leader to negotiate. But one fleet will not be enough. After we finish here I will move on to Yamamoto's fleet and try to add him to our ranks. Nicolette, I want you to take the Peacemaker to this solar system and look for something."

"What would that be?" She asked her sister.

"Old communication beacons. The space ships from two hundred years ago used to jettison the memory banks into computer storage canisters so that future space travelers could find them. I have a theory that the crew of the Calypso did that before Sikorsky blew them up. I want you to find those canisters, if they still exist, then broadcast them throughout the inter-solar system satellite communication broadcasts. If my theory is correct and the Andrews family left some form of warning behind, then the rest of humanity need to see it. It could act as a rallying cry to oust Sikorsky."

"And me?" Bennington asked. He had just begun a sexual relationship with Nicolette and did not want to be separated from her.

"You go with Nicolette. I need you to protect her," Penelope instructed. "With the fifty Replicants that are on each of the two Antony Super Raumschiffs, I will have enough man and woman power to do what needs to be done with the Second Fleet."

"When do we go?" Nicolette asked.

"Now," Penelope snapped her fingers again and a three dimensional view came up for the command crew of the Second Fleet ship named the *Montenegro*. "As you can see the Captain of this ship is a Sikorsky. Her executive officer, security chief, communications chief, weapons commander, chief pilot, three fighter pilot squadron commanders and two engineers are all Royal Family members. That is eleven of the highest ranking officers that we will need to kill to take the craft. The Montenegro is the closest to us so we will approach her first. We will knock out the crew and board as we did in the past. After we gather all of the eleven and eliminate them we will move on to the New Delhi and then the Rorke's Drift. The Nigeria and the Amistad will be last as they are the farthest from us."

"But the Amistad has Admiral Khan and Captain Allen on board. Shouldn't we take her first? If we convince Allen and Khan to join us they could order the other ships to stand down," Tucson Garrison suggested.

"That was my first thought as well. But no. We take the closest ship. Only this time we leave some of us behind to speak with the remaining officers to explain to them why we attacked. The Montenegro has a talented officer on board named Harvard. She is one of the daughters of the Dean of Clovis Academy. She is a Lieutenant Commander in Security and is a brilliant tactician. I want a few of the Drayton's to stay behind and wake her first. Explain the situation and see if she will join us or, in the alternative, not oppose us openly."

Drayton #0 touched the image of Harvard and the computer responded by showing a large view of her resume. "I can speak with her. Les Gillis and I were the two Gorski Gang members that Dean Harvard tolerated. I met his daughter a few years ago. She might remember me. Perhaps I can convince her to join us in total."

"That would be grand if you could," Penelope smiled at him. "Now. Let's take the Montenegro."

Nicolette hugged her sisters as she departed with

Bennington. After they were safely on their way aboard the *Peacemaker*, Penelope ordered that the two Raumschiffs loaned to her by Admiral Cardenas move into range of the *Montenegro*. The crew of that unsuspecting Battle Cruiser were rendered unconscious by the high frequency weapon which attacked the central nervous system. All of the crew fell to the floors of the six level war machine holding their ears. They were sleeping in seconds.

Penelope led her two ships to the docking port and boarded the larger space craft. They methodically located the eleven high ranking Royal Family officers and severed their heads from their bodies. Drayton #0 waited for Harvard to wake up. There was much for them to discuss.

Marco Andolini and Ellen Benson were serving on the five Battle Cruisers of the Second Fleet. They had both been assigned to the *Amistad* as patrol pilots. While the *Montenegro* was being taken over by Rosenburg and her followers, Marco and Benson were flying a twelve hour patrol mission, which was standard operating procedure for all Battle or Science Cruisers in deep space. Both Marco and Benson had been commissioned officer with the rank of Lieutenant Junior Grade and assigned their own Allen Type Fighter ship. They did not see the approach of the Super Raumschiffs near the *Montenegro*. The main reason was that the distance in space was too great. But the other reason was that Rosenburg and her small group of rebels were using advanced stolen alien technology to keep their ships invisible and non-detectable to the computer scans.

Marco and Benson found that being out in space to be peaceful to them. They loved the solace of the feeling of nothing around them save the hull of their space craft. As they flew in a tight formation together they spent hours speaking of all kinds of subjects. Between their long conversations and their sexual relationship that had become a regular occurrence between them, the two young officers were in love. The prospect of falling in love so quickly had not scared him as he had thought it might. He had been a playboy with hundreds of lovers due to his fame as a soccer player. But he had always admired his father, the way he stayed loyal to his wife for three decades. He equally looked up to his twin brother, Dominic, who found love with one of their class mates named Harumi. Dominic and Harumi seemed to evolve into an extension of one another. He had never seen his brother as happy as he was on the day of his wedding. Marco wanted that type of love and stability in his life. He thought he had found it once with a classmate named Mary Lincoln. But the relationship ended quickly and Marco was left alone to sort out his hurt feelings and broken heart.

When he found Benson was on the same Battle Cruiser, he gravitated to her. They had both survived the Blood Moon Incident and shared similar dreams and hopes. As they spent more and more time sharing dinners and drinks they became sexually active. Marco found that in addition to being brave and an excellent pilot, Benson was smart, possessed a great sense of humor and was generous with her body in the bedroom. She had a fiery disposition and was not one to cower away from a confrontation. All of those were qualities he found attractive in her.

"Ellen, how much longer until our shift ends?"

Benson checked her small clock on the command panel of her small Allen Type Fighter space craft. "We have two hours, my love. I am starving. How about you?"

"Famished. What would you like for dinner?"

"Dinner?" Benson chuckled. "Honey it is three in the morning. Dinner?"

"How about steak with eggs, hash browns, poggie bacon, some pancakes and a strawberry smoothie?" Marco asked out loud.

"I could eat my steering column right now. Why do they make our patrol shifts last so long? I heard that Dell pissed in her suit yesterday during her patrol. That cannot be easy to clean out of an enviro-suit."

Marco laughed. "That is probably why they make us wear adult diapers when we go on patrol. We don't make the regulations. Dell refused to wear the diapers. The CO will write her up for certain. Sucks to be her."

"We just follow orders. I know. I know."

"And after dinner or breakfast?" He asked her.

"Then we have each other for dessert," Benson told him with a devilish smile.

"I love you girl."

She laughed as he said it to her. She loved him as well. Hearing him tell her how he felt about her made her feel wonderful. She had never been happier in her life.

At the end of their flight shift, Marco and Benson were checked by the medical staff for any radioactive contamination and then cleared to enter the main body of their Battle Cruiser. The couple held hands as they walked up several levels to the third floor and the location of Take Ten. There were only about thirty patrons dining inside, a slow day for the bar. The crowd would increase when the time grew closer to six a.m. Marco led Benson to a grey table in the corner surrounded by four red cushioned chairs. Marco noticed that the majority of the other customers were medical or technical crewmembers.

Using her index fingers on the table top, Benson moved the menu into a three dimensional view, floating between her and Marco. The couple verbally ordered their breakfast into the computer communication micro-chip that was hidden inside the table. Gliding grey and black robotic waiters, looking eerily similar to humans, appeared with fresh coffee, cream, toast and jams. The couple thanked the mechanical servers and began to down their coffee as if they hadn't drank in weeks.

After downing a gulp of apple juice, Benson took his hand in hers and smiled. "So, Marco, my love, I have a serious question for you."

"Ask away."

"Why is it that a jocund, very sexy, talented and intelligent man like you never took on some wives? You must have had many women interested in you."

Marco leaned into the table and softly kissed Benson on her lips. He leaned back and gave her a serious look. "I was in love once with a woman so beautiful that words cannot describe her. She hurt me in every way a woman can hurt a man. After her, I just could not open my heart to anyone else. That is, until I met you. So to answer your question, yes I had many opportunities to take on some wives, but I opted not to."

"Tell me about her, the woman that broke your heart. I want to hear the entire story."

Marco shook his head, "Only Siobhan, Dom and Yuri know the whole story. They all witnessed what happened. Some of my sisters and a few other friends learned bits and pieces of it. I was in prep school, sixteen years old, a star on the Clovis City soccer team and I did have many women after me. Then I met Leeza. She was so radiant, beautiful and acted so sweet, innocent and understanding. She was older than me by two years and was working as a clerk for a municipal court near the capital buildings. She approached me at a coffee shop and before I knew it we were dating up a storm. She had a daughter named Chrissy."

"How old was Chrissy?"

"One. They lived with Leeza's parents which was how they avoided Chrissy being placed in one of the orphan homes. Their home was in the prestigious Meadow's Breeze area, full of multi-colored trees and a small lake that was stocked full of fish. I had to take one of the L-Tubes from my home to go see her. I was spending almost every evening at her place."

"So what happened?"

"I fell in love with her and grew to love her child as

if she were my own. Then Leeza began to show her true personality. I was told not to come over to her home without prior permission. She forbad me from visiting her at her office. She never wanted to have lunch with me. She even had to take business trips and would exclude me with the claim that it was for office employees only. As the months passed, I confided in Dom, Yuri, Siobhan, and some of the Evart sisters about how I was being treated. The consensus was that Leeza had another lover behind my back. So, I finally decided to start breaking her rules and going to her home unannounced, to her office and I started following her from a distance. I felt like a stalker."

"And what did you find out?"

"Well, one of my oldest friends, Carole Evart, contacted me with the news I had dreaded. Leeza was indeed sleeping with another man. It was her supervisor at her office. He was the reason I could not join Leeza on any of her business excursions. Carole was a pretty good sleuth and she learned that Leeza was meeting her boss at a hotel called Meadow's Peak. So, I went there with Carole and we waited in the lobby. Sure enough, Leeza and her boss showed up, arm in arm, laughing and kissing like folks in love would do. I confronted them. Leeza lied about the entire affair. By the way her boss reacted, it was clear that he knew all about me. He ran away like a coward. I suppose he was scared that I was going to beat him down."

"So what did you do?"

"I broke off everything with Leeza. I was heartbroken and felt lost. It took me months to get over her. I would often times take the L-Tube to the Meadow's Breeze subdivision just so I could catch a glimpse of Chrissy and make sure she was doing well. I still miss that little girl. I even considered filing in a family law court to get visitation rights but Yuri and Dom talked me out of it."

"So how did that experience stop you from marrying someone else?"

Marco sipped some of his coffee and leaned back in his chair as he thought out his next comments to her. "Look. I became a very bad man. After I got over the pain and the depression of losing Leeza, I dated hundreds of women and I slept with most of them. Sadly, the majority of them were really decent girls. I am certain that I hurt some of them. Every time I considered a serious relationship my mind would drift back to the cool wind of the Meadow's Breeze and I would just move on to the next girl, often times without an explanation to the prior one. I had two of the most prominent families really pissed off at me because I had allegedly deflowered one of their children. The Yutong's really hated me and I don't blame them."

"So if you are so damaged, why would you be willing to be loyal to me? I mean, since we have been on this ship together, you have slept with me exclusively. Why am I so special and all those other women were not?"

"Fair question. I suppose because I got over the pain and the memory of the depression that pain brought me. I learned through another short relationship that I was now emotionally ready for a commitment. I also watched two good friends of mine die on that Blood Moon. They were far too young to die and they both left behind loved ones. One of them had children and the other had a pregnant girlfriend waiting for him. I realized that life was far too short and that I was cheating myself by not opening heart to a good woman. Then I met you on the Blood Moon. I thought I would never see you again when I left to go home. Before I was assigned here, I watched my brother marry the sweetest girl. I saw the love in his eyes each time he looked at her. I wanted that for me. So, when I arrived on this ship and saw you serving here, I pursued you. As you know, I am physically attracted to you. You are smart, loyal and a close friend. I never told anyone else what happened to me with Leeza before. Only my closest childhood friends knew about it. I feel like with you, I never need to keep secrets. I can tell you everything about myself. I love you."

Benson smiled and took his hands in hers, "I love you, too. So, I have another question for you."

"Shoot."

"After we survived the attack by those jackanapes on the Blood Moon, did you even think that you and I would ever get together?"

Marco shook his head in the negative.

"So then our sleeping together was not due to some extravagant plot you came up with after you met me?"

"No. I'm not a stalker, if that is what you are getting at?"

"Not at all, Marco. It just seems so right, you understand? Being with you, Feeling your hands on my body while you make love to me. It feels like we were meant to be together."

"So what should we do about it?"

"Go back to my room after we eat and make love like there's no tomorrow."

"Sounds like a great idea."

CHAPTER TWO

Pravda Sikorsky loved visiting planet Earth. She especially enjoyed visiting the old museums and castles in Europe. Some of the castles were crumbling to the ground even after efforts to keep them in pristine condition. The many wars before the two hundred year rule of the Glorious Leader left much destruction and many wonderful artifacts were lost. Acid rain was another perpetrator that caused the slow demise of the ancient castles. But father time was the biggest culprit that caused the old massive stone castles to slowly decay. She found solace at some of the restaurants with their unique cuisines and menus. Each trip she made to Old Earth, she made it a point to eat a minimum of three meals a day at different restaurants to sample the tastes and enjoy the dining experience that each location had to offer.

But on this trip to Earth, Pravda was not on vacation. She would not have time to visit her favorite historical locations or wander aimlessly through a new museum to be exposed to ancient works of art. On this trip, she was on a mission for her family. Pravda had already finished her investigation into the beginnings of the current groundswell of anger against the Royal Family.

She had determined that the traitor came from the Rosenburg family. There were three of the female great great granddaughters of Vladimir Sikorsky missing. Pravda sent word to the Glorious Leader that those three should be hunted down and executed. The suspects were Penelope, Nicolette and Kristen Rosenburg. Pravda had visited Space Station Cy-7 and spoke with the person she had believed to be Penelope Rosenburg. Within thirty minutes, Pravda realized the Penelope she had met with was an imposter. Pravda made that conclusion as she scanned the fake Penelope and learned that there were no metallic implants on her bone structure. Penelope had been given numerous surgeries to make her taller and more beautiful than she could have ever dreamed.

Pravda had cut out the heart of the fake Penelope, left her dead in her office at the Baroness Hotel, and ransacked her offices for clues. Pravda located what she needed in the lower level storage units of the Hotel. She found large tubes that were known to her and her family.

They were not tubes for Cryogenic-Sleep. These were tubes to clone life forms from technology that had been stolen from an alien race called the Danaraja.

Pravda knew that the Rosenburg family had exclusive control over that technology as it was all located on the Rosenburg Ranch Territory of planet New Edinburgh. She also knew that there were only a few Rosenburg's that knew of the ability to clone and the fewer had the training to actually create successful cloned humans. Four were dead. The other four were accounted for. Two of the missing Rosenburg scientists that knew how to properly utilize the Danaraja machinery were Nicolette and Kristin Rosenburg.

After Pravda made her findings and informed the Glorious Leader, she was instructed to go to Earth for several missions. First, she was to deliver an ultimatum to several of the wealthiest families in the Empire. Second, she was directed to eliminate several of the politicians that were proving to be disloyal to the Royal Family. She had her list and gasped when she one of the names. The newly elected President of the Eastern European Province was slated for execution. Sikorsky knew the man well. His name was Janos Janicek, one of the Space Commands most decorated Admirals. Janicek had retired after over thirty years of service to the United Nations and returned to his home. He had been drafted by the people to run for their vacant leadership position. According to the reports, it looked like the elder Admiral had not quashed the rebellions that were building up in Poland, Hungary and Rumania. The Glorious Leader expected the regional leaders to keep the people in line. For failing to do so, Janicek had to die. Pravda immediately boarded her Super Raumschiff called the *Princess Death* and plotted her course for Earth.

Pravda guided her ship into the Earth atmosphere and set herself on a landing scheme toward Houston, Texas Territory. Texas Territory was the largest land mass of the defunct United States. When the federal government spent itself into oblivion, the fifty states of that union broke apart to form separate nation states. Texas had merged with the states called Oklahoma, New Mexico and Arizona and took in the Mexican state of Chihuahua to form the Texas Territory. It was the wealthiest and most prosperous of the territories that had once been a part of the United States of America.

Houston, Texas was the home of the wealthy and powerful industrialist Fenster family. Centuries earlier, the Fenster's bought out the former buildings and research, documents and designs of the organization known as NASA. The Fenster's owned all of what the former United States had as their space program. The Fenster's advanced the research and knowledge of that former space agency to grow into one of the most influential manufacturing concerns of space craft for all of humanity. The Fenster's expanded their business endeavors into weaponry, space suits, cryogenics, suspended animation, solar power, developing hybrid engines and power sources and construction projects.

Pravda personally liked the Fenster family for all of the advancements they had brought to humanity, and had reservations being the one to deliver them a threat from the Royal Family. She had admired their standards of excellence when it came to space ship design and engineering as well as their attempts to keep life simplistic at home. Most of their mansion was surrounded by farm land full of crops, open ranges for their cattle and stables for hundreds of horses. Pravda found the Fenster way of life to be agreeable with the way she had hoped to live out her retirement.

Morgan Fenster, III, was the current Chief Executive officer of the Fenster Corporation. He was in his late sixties, still handsome and fit as if he were a man in his twenties. He had taken over the large corporate concern when he was in his forties when his father handed the power over to him. Fenster had many sons and daughters as well as numerous grandchildren. His wife of forty-two years, Blanca, was his closest friend and confidant. Blanca was a corporate lawyer and had been working for the Fenster family when she met Morgan. They were married in less than a year after that initial meeting.

Morgan Fenster, III, had been at the bed side of his grandfather, also named Morgan, who was dying from a rare bone disease. Morgan Fenster had reached the age of one hundred nineteen before his body began to fail him. The family brought the old man to his mansion home outside of Houston, Texas so that he could die in the comforts of his bed room.

Pravda spied through the windows of the spacious mansion and observed Morgan Fenster, III, locating his wife in one of the several kitchens of the eight floor, ninety-seven room mansion. He kissed Blanca on the lips.

"Good morning my love," Morgan, III, greeted her.

"Buenas," Blanca Rodriguez Fenster responded. "How is Papa?" Papa was the loving name Blanca had given to the elder Morgan Fenster.

"Not good," her husband responded as he poured a

cup of coffee for himself. "He hardly recognizes me anymore. The end will be soon."

Blanca hugged him, "We all love him. At least when he passes he will not suffer any longer."

Morgan kissed his wife on the forehead. "I know. I miss him so much. Just a few months ago he seemed so alive, so vibrant and this disease takes him."

"Yes, very sad." It was a strange voice that they heard behind them. The Fenster couple turned to face the person in their mansion home. They did not recognize her. But she was not alone as there was another woman with her, also a complete stranger.

"Who the hell..." Morgan began, his voice was angry. His son, Morgan, IV, was in charge of security for the mansion and had clearly failed in his job.

"Relax. Drink your coffee," the woman told them. "My name is Pravda Sikorsky. I am part of the Royal Family. My friend here is Ulla Ragnarsson. We have a message to deliver to you and your family."

"Royal or not, how did you get in here? What are you wanting from us? This is private property and you have no right to be here unless invited." Blanca went into her lawyer attack mode.

"Calm down. We have a message to deliver."

Pravda motioned to Ulla. "Show them the photographs."

Ulla was holding a nine inch by twelve inch manila folder in her right hand. She handed it over to Blanca. The woman opened the folder and gasped in horror. She showed the photographs to her husband. He dropped his coffee cup to the floor and stood in silence as it shattered to several pieces, coffee spattering in every direction. The pictures were of three of their grandchildren, Dirk, Therese and Frederick. All three were shown handcuffed, in their underwear in a strange cell.

"Is this about money?" Morgan raised his voice in anger. "Where are they?"

"What have you done to them?" Blanca was distraught, her voice cracking.

"Calm down, you will live longer. They are all three alive and well." Ulla smiled at the man in an effort to calm him. "We do not want money. Only, your cooperation."

"Cooperation for what? What do you want from us?" Blanca pleaded, holding a picture of Dirk and Therese in her trembling hands.

Pravda pointed out the window, "You see out there, in the real world, there is a war beginning. There are those that wish to end the rule of the Glorious Leader. We want both of you and all of your family to give us your corporation, your influence and your power to all side with maintaining the rule of Vladimir Sikorsky. You do that, your three grandchildren will live long and happy lives."

"And if we don't?" Morgan asked the question he already knew the answer to. "How can we trust you? You come into our home, uninvited, and make demands on us by threatening our family. Who do you think you are?"

Pravda shook her head menacingly. "Do not refuse us. You take any overt actions against my family, then I will bring back the head of one of your three precious grandchildren. You defy us a second time, I will return with the second head. You do understand where we are going with this?"

The Fenster's looked into each other's eyes. They were educated people, kept up with current events and were well informed regarding the recent insurrections in the Nevada Territory, the Eastern European Province and Ireland. Until now, the Fenster family had decided to remain neutral. Governmental change was not a priority to them. They were wealthy beyond the majority of the population and owed a great part of their success to the regime of Sikorsky. They had never been treated adversely by those in power. But now, with this threat putting them under duress to protect the lives of their grandchildren, the Fenster's were livid. They had no choice but to do as these women were demanding. But this move by the Sikorsky's would irreparably harm their willingness to be so trusting with the current leaders in the future. But for the moment, they would do as they were asked.

"We will cooperate," Morgan told her.

"Good," Pravda smiled. "I knew you were reasonable people. I am glad. The one with the dark hair, Dirk? I think he is very handsome. I would rather become his lover than his executioner. What do you think? Would Dirk be attracted to a woman like me?"

Blanca glared at the woman. In her legal career, Blanca had to quickly determine what kind of people she was dealing with. In the few moments of interaction with this Pravda Sikorsky, Blanca concluded she was clearly a sociopath. "Miss, can you just tell us where our grandchildren are? Can we speak to them?"

"I cannot let you speak to them. Not yet." Pravda answered. "The Glorious Leader has plans to crush all of the rebellions, one by one. He plans on doing it in a manner that will dissuade anyone in the future from dissenting to his rule. Once that occurs and everything goes back to normal, we will let you know where Dirk, Therese and

Frederick are being held. You have my word that they will be returned to you safely."

Dirk Fenster felt as if a horse had bashed in his skull. He had never had such a horrible, throbbing, headache in his life. Not even from his many hang overs from the holiday and weekend adventures he shared with Arch Frazier and the other Gorski Gang members. He was in a bed, with no mattress or pillow. The bed was a cold, solid grey metal. Dirk sat up and inspected his surroundings, he was in a blue colored ten foot by ten foot by ten foot high room. He was wearing a pair of thermal pants. He had no shirt on, nor shoes or socks. His mouth was dry, as if he had not drank water for days.

Dirk sat up in his bed, massaging both sides of his head with his hands. He was trying to recall what had happened. He was at the party for Dean Harvard. There was a gas leak of some sort. He remembered standing up to run. He was stunned by a laser blast, of that much he was certain. Then he wakes up here, in what was clearly a prison cell of some sort.

He stood up and began to search the walls with his hands, hoping to find a crack in the wall. Anything.

Then he heard the voice.

"Good, you are awake." It was a male voice, with a

Russian accent from what Dirk could tell. He looked around him and realized that the ceiling must have many hidden cameras for security. He was being watched by his captors.

"Who are you?" Dirk yelled out to the voice. "Where am I?"

"I am Vladimir Sikorsky, Junior. I am your, how should I say, your host? Yes, your host for your stay with us. You can call me Junior! Everyone else does!"

"Can you show yourself? I prefer to speak with people face to face."

"Why of course, my friend," the Sikorsky voice responded.

Dirk watched as the wall to his left opened, allowing bright light to enter the room that he was in. As the walls slid sideways they revealed a hallway outside of his room. Dirk saw that several other sliding doors were opening up and down the large hallway. He ran to the opening and was grateful he was not stopped by some invisible force field. The hallway had a ceiling that was about fifteen feet high. The floors were a shade of blue, the walls were red. He began walking toward one of the other open doorways.

He watched as a very beautiful blonde haired woman stepped out into the hallway. She was wearing a white bra and a pair of the same thermal pants that Dirk had on.   The girl looked at him, her light blue eyes wide with fear. Dirk also looked the woman over. He deduced that she was a prisoner, just as he was.

"Who are you?" The woman asked, her voice full of fear and doubt. Dirk could see that the girl had been crying just before she walked out into the hallway. She was covering her full breasts by folding her arms over them.

"My name is Dirk. Dirk Fenster. Who are you?"

"I am Christian Allen," the girl answered as she backed up against the wall. She was giving him a suspicious look. "You and your family did this to me? Are you going to kill me because of what you blame my family for?"

Dirk held his hands up, waving at her. "No. No. I am not your enemy here. We are both prisoners of a Vladimir Sikorsky, Junior."

"The son of the Glorious Leader!" Christian Allen began laughing hysterically. "Really? You expect me to believe that? You Fenster's are ridiculous. You call my uncle Bruce a murderer, make his life hell, accuse my family of all kinds of things, and now you want revenge by taking us hostage?"

"Us? What us? Are there more of you?" Dirk demanded.

"Yes, my sisters." Christian pointed back into the room she had walked out of. "Esther and Angelica. They are still asleep."

"Therese!" Dirk realized that if someone was taking hostages of the wealthy families, his sister was as good a target as he was. He ran into one of the other rooms and found, just as he had feared, his sister Therese, asleep on the metallic bed. She was dressed just as Christian Allen, in a bra and thermal pants. Dirk cradled her lovingly in his arms and checked her pulse. To his relief, Therese was alive.

Christian Allen was standing in the doorway, watching him with confusion on her face. "Who is she?"

"My sister, Therese. She's breathing. Where are we? Are there others with us?"

Christian nodded, watching how Dirk held his sister. Christian had been told stories her whole life that the Fenster's were cold hearted and hateful people. The behavior she observed out of the one called Dirk suggested otherwise. He was very loving in the way held his sister.

Christian cleared her throat, "Well we are not alone.

The cell across from me has two women. Two other cells had a man in each. I think that was all I saw."

"And that is all that there is," the Russian accented voice boomed from the hallway.

Dirk stood and followed Christian out into the hallway. They both saw a man in royal red and purple robes, standing about six feet tall. His dark hair was shiny from oils. He was wearing several gold necklaces and had a ring on every finger. Surrounding him were seven Marines, in Class C uniforms.

"Welcome to the United Nations Space Command Battle Cruiser Waterloo of the First Fleet," Junior Sikorsky said proudly. "I am the son of the Glorious Leader. I am your host. The other three guests are two Breckenridge children, a Brackenridge boy and one of your cousins. His name is Frederick Fenster. They will all be awake soon."

Junior Sikorsky was only a few years shy of his two hundredth birthday. He, like his father and other family members, used metallic implants and body parts from innocent women to obtain immortality. Junior Sikorsky looked over the body of Christian Allen and licked his lips. He enjoyed raping his body part donors and then hearing their screams as his surgeons removed their kidneys or liver or heart. The best screams were when they sliced off the victim's skin with sharp surgical tools. Since the Marines were there to protect him, Sikorsky contemplated raping this Christian Allen right then and there. But, he knew he had to wait until the rebellion was crushed. Then he could violate the Allen woman and carve her to pieces.

Dirk was grinding his teeth and he had crossed his arms. He was certain that the Empire was behind this. His father had always taught young Dirk to be wary of authority, especially the Glorious Leader. Dirk found out that his father had been right when the Rosenburg family had sent assassins out to kill his closest friends. "Why are we all here?"

"To keep your families honest," Junior laughed. "You eight youngsters are our insurance that your families will not get involved."

"Get involved with what?" Christian's tone of voice was angry, and she was no longer scared or timid. She was concerned at how the Sikorsky man was looking her over.

"The civil war," Sikorsky said simply. "There are those that are demanding that the Glorious Leader step down. Some of the many planets in the eight solar system have begun to declare their independence. The situation cannot be allowed to continue. All of those involved in the insurrections must die as an example to the average that the rule of my father is perpetual and cannot be challenged. We will win the war. Very soon, in fact. Once the conflict is over all of you will be allowed to go home."

"What war?" Dirk demanded, he wondered how long he had been unconscious.

"We will take all of you to another holding area," Sikorsky informed them, ignoring Dirk's question. "We will give you access to broadcast screens so you can watch the world events as they unfold. You will be fed well. So, relax. This ship is safe. Soon you will all be reunited with your families."

Dirk grunted at that. He knew his cousin Frederick was a wild one, with a history of juvenile troubles and illegal drug consumption. He had been arrested for many assaults, beating a police officer, thefts and he had stolen a Raumschiff and crashed it into a flat field. Once he was an adult, Frederick had beaten another police officer, started three bar fights and had begun selling Red Dust to make money after the family cut off his allowance monies. Once the captors on this ship informed Frederick Fenster he was not free to leave, there would be a riot on board the *Waterloo.*

Sikorsky motioned for the two to follow him to the elevator lift as some of his Marine Corps guards collected the unconscious Allen girls, Therese and Frederick Fenster and the two Breckenridge women. Dirk followed obediently, hoping that his friends and family were searching for them. He was certain escape from a full-fledged Battle Cruiser would be next to impossible. To make matters worse, even if by some miracle he could find a way off the ship for himself and his fellow captives, they would be dead in no time from the firepower that the *Waterloo* most certainly possessed.

Dirk could hear Junior Sikorsky babbling on and on about his role in the Akarzdamedian Wars and following his father into battle. Dirk kept his mouth shut and humored the old man, listening to him relate his past glories as they waited for the Marines to carry the other prisoners into the elevator. He wondered whether he would be able to get his host to offer any information that might prove as useful to developing a plan to escape.

"The Waterloo, it was not around during the Racial Wars?" Dirk played dumb, as he knew that the *Waterloo* was a newer version of the Battle Cruiser Class of space craft.

"Oh no!" Sikorsky laughed out loud. "No! The Waterloo was built just fifteen years ago. It is one of the state of the art Battle Cruisers."

"So the crew would be much more than the Class of ships that were around at the time of the Akarzdamedian Wars?"

"Correct!" Sikorsky was pointing his finger at the ceiling for dramatic effect. "The Waterloo has a crew of just under eighteen hundred men and women. Mostly pilots, weapons operatives and Marines. The hull of the ship is triple plated with varying metal alloys..." Sikorsky stopped speaking and looked at Dirk and Christian quizzically. He began laughing out loud again. "But you two already know these things! Your families built almost all of the ships in the entire Space Command!"

Dirk caught Christian giving him an odd look, as if she did not understand why he would engage their kidnapper in polite chit chat. Dirk's intent was to get the man to give him all the free information possible so that he could use it later to escape, if possible. The elevator stopped moving and the doors slid open to reveal a long hallway with a new set of doorways on the left and right. Sikorsky motioned for them to follow him into the hall. Dirk walked out behind the attractive Allen woman and the guards carrying the other hostages were the last out of the elevator. Sikorsky led them all to the ninth door on the right, which was already open, and motioned for them to enter.

Dirk walked in first as Christian hesitated. The room was twenty-five feet wide and thirty feet long. The ceilings were about twenty feet high. The far wall was not a wall at all but an observation window. Dirk and Christian could see the binary star system in the great distance and a planet with three moons closer. Dirk immediately deduced that the planet was Sikorsky's Planet. He looked at the different angles to locate the space stations but they were not visible from the angle of their room. There were four sets of three level bunk beds in the room on the east wall. The west wall had a shower with a curtain, a toilet and a sink. There was one grey metal table in the center of the room, welded into the floor, with ten red plastic chairs around it.

Dirk pulled one of the chairs out for Christian to sit down in. The two watched as the Marines placed the other hostages on the bunk beds. The soldiers then stood at parade rest as Sikorsky sat down in front of the two hostages.

"This is your home away from home." Sikorsky was nodding his head up and down as if to drive the point with authority to them. "It is very comfortable. You will all be well fed. Near the showers are Class C uniforms for your use. They are all sized to fit each one of you. We will broadcast here, on the center of this table, all of the news reports of the war. You will also observe, no doubt, some actual battles from these observation windows."

"You're expecting a battle here?" Dirk probed, pointing at the observation window.

"Absolutely," Sikorsky smiled and stood up. "Enjoy the view of space.   The binary star system is magnificent, is it not?"   Without waiting for an answer, Sikorsky stood and walked out of the room with his Marines in escort. The doors to the room slid shut.

"Why are you being nice to him?" Christian demanded.

"Because you attract more bees with honey." Dirk stood and ran to the windows and tried to locate the space stations of the rest of the First Fleet. He could not see any of the ships or stations. He had studied the star charts and solar systems in his Introduction to Astral Navigation course at Clovis Academy. He would recognize the view before him in his sleep. "You know where we are?"

"Yes," Christian responded and was soon standing next to him. "What are you thinking?"

"That we are being watched and our conversation is being monitored," Dirk told her quickly so she would not blurt out any of her thoughts regarding any plans of fleeing the ship. "Our only hope is that our families will find us. There is no escape."

Dirk walked over toward the lone shower stall and began fumbling with the uniforms that were there. Each was a one piece with a gold zipper running up the center of the red colored outfit. There were also some red slippers lying on the floor for the hostages. He found one that had his size etched on the interior of the suit at the neck line.

"All you can think about at a time like this is to dress up in those things?" Christian demanded of him. "We have to get off this ship! We have to get out of here!"

Dirk walked over to her and took her hands in his. She was sounding hysterical and needed to get control of herself. "Calm down. We can only take care of things that we can take care of now. He said the First Fleet, which is Admiral Perdicas' Fleet. He is another child of the Glorious Leader. His mother was one of the heroes of the Akarzdamedian Wars and one of the wives of the Glorious Leader. The First Fleet has only one mission, to protect Sikorsky's Planet, her moons and space stations. They have some of the best trained soldiers in the Space Command.

There is no escape."

"So we just take it?" Christian demanded.

"No, right now you shower." Dirk pointed to the shower stall. "You better be quick about it, because my cousin Frederick will probably go wild if he sees a pretty girl like you naked in a shower. And by wild I mean he will be uncontrollable. While you shower, think long and hard about our situation and you need to learn to keep your thoughts to yourself. You need to realize that we are in a very bad position here and we all need to be smart, alert and work together if we are going to survive this."

Christian glared at him, "My family was right about you people. We should be planning to get away. All you want to do is cooperate with these thugs? You disgust me, Fenster!" She turned away from him and walked toward the shower. "I hope you will be gentleman enough to turn your back while I undress."

Dirk shrugged and walked over to the large observation windows. "Do not worry about me. Save your venom for the real villains in this."

As Christian showered, Dirk stared out the observation window and he began to ponder what Yuri Gorski, Julia Steiner or Les Gillis would do if they were in the same situation. They were nine hostages inside a ship with about eighteen hundred well trained soldiers. There could not be any escape, but he began to formulate a plan to do just that. Yuri and his friends had taught Dirk that anything was possible, even the impossible. Yuri had been able to keep the majority of his team alive on the Blood Moon. They did so against impossible odds. Dirk determined that he would succeed in not escaping his captors, but in killing them all and stealing their ship. He began to formulate in his mind the various scenarios that he could put in place to pull off the greatest coup in history. Nine against eighteen hundred, trapped inside a metal Battle Cruiser in the middle of a hostile solar system of ten planets and over fifty moons full of loyal soldiers that would hunt them to the death. Not good odds for what he was planning. He stared out at the darkness of outer space and wondered about his friends and his Timber Wolf, Theodora. He hoped that no harm had found them.

CHAPTER THREE

Lieutenant Junior Grade Marco Andolini stirred in his bed. He had slept well during the night. Sleeping next to him was his newest love, Ellen Benson. She held the same rank as Marco and was a fellow member of the Space Command as pilots aboard the U.N.S.C. Battle Cruiser *Amistad* of the Second Fleet.

Marco and Benson had not been assigned as wing partners but they were part of the same forty-two person flight squadron. The *Amistad* was the same war ship class as the Battle Cruiser *Cortez*. She had six levels with a crew of one thousand five hundred men and women. There were several married service men and women and their spouses and children were also part of the passenger list which gave the total population on board to just under two thousand. The *Amistad* was the flag ship of the Second Fleet. In addition to the Amistad, the Second Fleet consisted of four other Battle Cruisers, the *Rorke's Drift*, the *New Delhi*, the

Montenegro and the *Nigeria*. The ships were all built as war machines, complete with armor piercing rockets, lasers batteries, fifty Raumschiff's in the upper docking bays and seven hundred fifty Allen Corporation Fighter Type CC76A3 space ships.

Marco and Benson had been two of the so-called heroes of the Blood Moon Incident. On their first night of their new service on their first assignment as officers, Marco and Benson sought each other out. They had stayed in constant computer communication with each other since they met on the Moon of Semiramis. They were very much attracted to one another. Marco had found her courage to be a quality he desired in a companion. They shared dinner and drinks together on their first night on the *Amistad* and then they made love for the first time. In the months that followed they had been together every free moment.

Benson was still sleeping as Marco slid out of bed to take a shower. He did his best not to wake her. Benson had patrol duty in a few hours and needed the extra sleep. Their ship's Captain, Bruce Allen, had about a dozen small one man space fighter ships on patrol at all times. Captain Allen seemed a bit paranoid, claiming that the ship's scientific advances had scanning abilities were superb, but the human eye could detect things in space that science could not. So, for security purposes, Captain Allen had the patrols going out twenty-four hours a day. Each patrol was an eight hour shift. Marco had done several since joining the Amistad. He was cognizant of how taxing the boring flight patrols could be.

And how tiring.

Accordingly, Marco allowed Benson the extra hour or two of sleep. After he finished his shower, he dried off and dressed into his Class C flight uniform and sat down at his desk. He quietly prompted his computer to show him his e-mails. The three dimensional view of about thirty unread messages appeared to float in the sky before him. He found a message from his twin brother, Dominic. Marco quickly read the letter which updated him on how Dominic, Yuri Gorski and Drew Harrison were doing on the *Cortez*. Marco quickly typed out a response on his three dimensional, holographic keypad. He wished his brother and his friends well. Marco missed them all terribly. Marco and Dominic came from a huge sibling group, from which they were the oldest. Many of their younger siblings had just entered the Clovis Academy, to follow in their footsteps. Thanks to the wonders of technology, the Andolini siblings were able to keep in touch through computer transmissions that bounced off of thousands of satellites in the distance between them.

Marco was about to read a message from another of his brothers, Lucius, when the *Amistad* shook violently. The klaxons of from the Security Section began blaring loudly. Benson jumped to her feet, her eyes wide with fear and her heart pounding in her chest. Marco was also upright looking around his quarters, expecting to see a hull breach or some other evidence of an explosion.

He saw none.

"What the hell?" Benson demanded.

Marco heard the security broadcast informing the crew that the *Amistad* was under attack from the inside. "Intruder alert! Intruder Alert!" The ship's computer announced loudly over the screaming alarms. "Multiple intruders on decks five, four, two and one. Security please respond!"

"We are being invaded!" Marco yelled over the shrieking klaxons.

Benson began throwing on her flight suit uniform as Marco readied their utility belts, checking their hand laser charges so they could be prepared to fight back.

The ship shook again, causing both Benson and Marco to fall to their left and hit the floor. They heard explosions from the inside of the ship.

"Sounds like the fighting is out in our hall way!" Marco yelled as he stood to his feet.

"I think you are right!" Benson stood up, her left arm braced against the wall of Marco's quarters. She had recently learned she was pregnant with Marco's child and had been waiting for the right moment to tell him the news. She prayed that the fall did not harm the fetus. Marco helped Benson steady herself and he put her utility belt on her.

"I am going out there," Marco told her.

"No, Marco." Benson was afraid of losing the man. Over the months of their relationship, she had fallen in love with him. She could not fathom what her life would be like if he was not a part of it.

"Relax mi amor," Marco said softly. He kissed her on the lips. "We need to know what is happening outside."

Benson watched as he ran to his quarter's entrance and put his back against the wall. He was one foot to the left of his doorway. Marco drew his laser pistol and aimed at his door.

"Computer, open the door!" Marco commanded. The door slid open as he had ordered. He saw laser fire in the corridor outside his quarters going in each direction. He could hear some screams outside as well. The metal walls and floor of the hallway had scorch marks from laser fire. Thankfully, there were no people standing just outside the door. But down the hallway, he saw several Marines and Military Intelligence personnel advancing, firing their laser rifles at targets on the opposite end of the corridor. One of the men in a black Class C uniform saw the open door and ran toward it and slid inside.

Marco recognized the man as First Lieutenant Shinghi Khan, the son of the Admiral of the Fleet. Marco reached out with his free arm and helped Khan inside the room. By now, Benson was fully dressed and standing next to him. Benson had her laser pistol in her left hand, her eyes darting back and forth, ready for any intruder to attempt to enter their room. Marco noted that Khan's uniform had a few slashes through the long sleeves and his collar. Shinghi Khan was a brave man, and a trained fighter from India on Old Earth. His father was Admiral of the Second Fleet Rajesh Khan. The Admiral was rumored to be over one hundred years old, kept alive with several mechanical body parts including metallic bones in his legs and hips. The Admiral had a dozen wives and many children with each woman. Shinghi was a part of a sibling group that served in several locations for the Space Command. Their family had made military service a family tradition.

"Thanks, Marco!" Khan said loudly over the klaxons and laser fire.

"What the hell is happening?" Benson demanded to know. "Is this some unannounced drill?"

"We were boarded," Khan stood up and aimed his laser rifle out the door. "Someone knew our security codes. The top ranking officers on the other four ships of our fleet were attacked. They're all dead. The crews of the other ships have been captured. Captain Allen and my father are on the Command Station directing the fight."

"The other ships? You mean the other four Battle Cruisers of our Fleet?" Marco asked. "How could such a thing happen?"

Khan nodded, "You catch on fast. They took over the Rorke's Drift, the New Delhi, the others. They were all attacked from the inside. The remaining crew members on all four battle cruisers have announced that they have pledged allegiance to their invaders."

Marco and Benson looked at each other with confused expressions. They knew that such an act would be treason and punishable by death. "They did what?" Both Marco and Benson asked in unison.

Marco worried about the fate of Dia Cho and

Felicia Essex who were Weapons Officers on board one of the other Battle Cruisers. Cho and Essex would not back down from a fight and if their ship had capitulated then that would not bode well for the two women. Marco also worried for the four children of Cho and Essex. He hoped that these invaders were merciful to innocent children.

There was more laser fire. Blasts were impacting the metallic walls outside Marco's quarters.

Marco observed two Marines fall to the metallic floor of the corridor outside his door. Khan was firing his laser rifle down the hallway.

"Can you help me?" Khan said more as an order than request.

Marco nodded and leaned out his door and aimed to his left at the attackers. He gasped when he got a look at the four men at the other end of the walkway. Marco leaned back inside his room. Khan did the same when he realized that Marco was not covering him.

"What the hell is wrong with you Lieutenant?" Khan demanded. "We need to fight back. They are the enemy."

"No, they can't be the enemy." Marco swallowed hard. It was impossible. "I know them. I mean him."

"Who are they?" Khan yelled.

"Drayton Love-Easter," Marco sighed. The sight of his old friend and fellow Gorski Gang member out in the hallway, shooting at Marines and MI soldiers left Marco in a state of bewilderment. Further, he was certain that Drayton Love-Easter had no twins in his sibling group. They spent many hours together discussing their families. Love-Easter had never been one to hold back a fact such as being a part of four identical twins. "Four of them. How can that be? He had no twins and none of his siblings resembled him so closely. He was loyal to the service. Why would he attack a Battle Cruiser?"

Khan watched as more of his Marines fell to the laser fire. "If you know them, can you tell me how to fight back? They are slaughtering my men!"

"He is a member of Spetsnaz," Marco began. "He was one of the best marksmen and hand to hand fighters at my Academy. If that really is Drayton Love-Easter out there, he will not lose."

"Well, if we can't fight him," Khan said thoughtfully, "will he listen to reason?"

"You mean will he negotiate?"

"Yes. Will he talk?"

"I will try to see what he, what they, want." Marco handed his hand laser to Benson. He partially wanted to see what he could do to cease the hostilities. But he was primarily curious as to how there were multiple Love-Easter's on the ship. "I will be back honey."

"Where do you think you are going?" Benson glared at him.

"Out there," Marco pointed out toward the corridor littered with unconscious Marines and MI soldiers.

"And you think they won't shoot you down like all of them?" Benson motioned to the bodies on the floor. There had to be dozens.

"I have to try," Marco kissed her on the cheek. "You should try to have more faith."

Marco walked over to the doorway and shouted as loud as he could. "Marines, back off!"

The Marines ignored Marco and kept firing.

"Marines!" Khan cut in. "You were ordered to back off by an officer! Do it!"

The Marines began to withdraw from the melee and back down the hallway. Marco smiled as the behavior was typical. The Marines never liked taking orders from Space Command pilots. But since Khan was MI, they listened to him.

Marco cleared his throat, "Dray! If that is you, it's me, Marco Andolini!" He was screaming at the top of his lungs. "Will you cease fire so I can come out and talk with you?"

"Marco," came the response after a few seconds. "Come on out. We will call a cessation to hostilities for you, my friend."

Marco nodded to Khan and Benson. He was laughing as if there were some inside joke. "It is Dray. I would recognize his voice anywhere." Marco winked at Benson. "Dray! I am coming out!"

Marco stepped out into the corridor and stepped over one of the Marines. He had both of his hands up in the air, to demonstrate that he was unarmed. He could not believe that his friend, Drayton Love-Easter, would kill all of these men and women. He quickly counted about twenty-five down.

He looked down the hall and saw four Drayton Love-Easter's looking back at him. "No one is dead," one of the Love-Easter's announced. "We just stunned them all."

Marco kept walking toward the four men. He recalled that Love-Easter had left to planet New Berlin with his wife Yesenia Guevara and their son. The whole scene before him was impossible. It must be a nightmare, he told himself. He noticed that the klaxons had stopped blaring.

There was an eerie silence over the large space craft. He could hear only the sounds of his boots on the metal floor as he moved closer and closer to the four Drayton Love-Easter's. He finally got within three feet of them. Marco looked each of the men over. They were exactly the same, like four perfect twins.

"How can this be?" Marco asked of them.

"No hugs?" one of the Drayton Love-Easter's asked, smiling as he recalled the normal pattern of the Andolini brothers hugging their friends as a form of greeting. "Marco, I know you must have many questions. I am Drayton Love-Easter #8. Behind me are #9, #10 and #11. We are exact duplicates of the real Drayton Love-Easter. There are many of us now, a whole army worth. We each possess the DNA, the memories and knowledge of the real Love-Easter. You could call us clones, duplicates, replicants, copies or any other term you wish. But we are each Drayton Love-Easter."

Marco began rubbing the palms of his hands on his cheeks. It had to be a nightmare. "How? How did you get...copied?"

Love-Easter #9 spoke now, "The real Love-Easter died on Space Station Cy-7. The woman you know as Penelope Smith was really Penelope Rosenburg. She and two of her sisters collected Love-Easter's DNA and were able to down load his memories and brain patterns to a computer diskette. They created all of us in some advanced alien replication tubes."

"Jesus! The Rosenburg's are in on this!" Marco bellowed in anger. The fact that the real Drayton had really died did not shock Marco as he had been suspicious of the cover story that he was in a coma and not dead. Marco had been told by witnesses that Drayton had his throat slashed. He would have bled out in minutes. "Those bastard's tried to kill all of us on the Blood Moon. They ambushed us twice at the Academy! What the hell are they up to now?"

Love-Easter #8 put his hand on Marco's shoulder, "Marco, these three Rosenburg women are up to one thing only. They wish to bring freedom to every person and alien life form in the eight solar systems. They are starting a revolution against the Glorious Leader."

"That is treason!" Marco's eyes widened. "And you? You are a part of it?"

"As should you be, my friend," Love-Easter #10 responded. "The Rosenburg's that tried to kill you, Yuri, Les and the others are Sikorsky's. They are members of the Royal Family. Do you not recall the assassins they sent in after you during the dust storm? Do you remember the attack from the ship called the Blitzkrieg? You led Tina Martinson and Roy Starr to their deaths to defend others. Remember? How about Dark October when several assassins killed some of the families of the ranking officers of New Edinburgh?"

Marco looked away as he recalled how the two cadets died. He had always felt a measure of personal responsibility for what had happened to them.

"They will never die and they will maintain power over all of humanity in perpetuity unless they are stopped," Love-Easter #11 said.

Marco shook his head, "No way. This cannot be."

"Marco, I remember years ago you told me a story about your aunt, on Mars, wasn't it?" Love-Easter #8 said. "You told me she and her whole family were killed by the Sikorsky assassins when she began to speak out against the policies of the Glorious Leader. Do you remember telling me of that?"

Marco covered his mouth. He had only told Mary Johnson Lincoln and Drayton Love-Easter of those events. This was no trick. Standing before him were truly copies of his dear friend. "I remember. We were drunk and I told you when we were watching the stars above us that night. They killed my aunt, uncle and my cousins. My cousins were children. The oldest was six and they killed them all."

"And they killed the real Drayton. They killed Pierre Zerbe and Porfirio Cardenas. They killed Tina Martinson and Roy Starr. They have killed hundreds, thousands, of others," Love-Easter #9 said calmly. "The ship's alarms have ended, my friend. That means my brothers in arms have taken control of the ship. Join us, Marco. Bring the brave Lieutenant that we saw dive into your quarters. He was a worthy adversary and would be a great asset to the fight for freedom. And if you are still the same Marco I remember, bring the girl in your room with you."

"How do you know I have a girl in my room?" Marco demanded.

"Because you are Marco Andolini, one of the stars of the Clovis City Rattlesnakes soccer team. You always had women, they flock to you." Love-Easter #8 was smiling. "Call them to join us on the Command Station. All will be made known to you then. Please, my friend."

"And after we hear you out and we decide not to join your rebellion, do you then kill us all?" Marco was still skeptical.

"We will not kill anyone else," Love-Easter #10 promised. "You will all be free to leave the ship in peace if you do not wish to participate in the liberation of humanity from the tyranny of the Glorious Leader. There are no conditions on your attendance."

"So, the Love-Easter that married Yesenia Guevara was a replica?" Marco concluded.

"Yes, he was. One of us had to make things right for her and the child," Love-Easter #8 explained. "Guevara and her son were innocent. They both deserved to have a good life. One of our brothers took the place of the original Love-Easter. You must promise to never reveal this. Guevara and her son must always believe that the man with them is the one and only Drayton."

"Okay," Marco recalled the look of joy in Guevara's eyes when she married what everyone believed to be Drayton Love-Easter. She had been so happy.

Marco looked back down the hallway, "Ellen, Shinghi! Come on out! They wish to take us to the Level One to continue the discussion. It will be alright."

Benson and Khan slowly walked out into the hallway. They both had their weapons in their hands, just in case.

Love-Easter #9 laughed, "We were right, you did have a girl in your room. Damn, Marco. She's a hottie. You still have it. How did you meet her? Does she have any sisters?"

Marco ignored all of the questions from the Love-Easter clones and waited for Benson and Khan to join them before stepping onto the ship's lift system. Marco took the time to look closely at each of the four Love-Easter's. They looked, sounded, acted and were just like the real thing. Marco could not wait to hear the truth behind all of this.

The lift shot upwards at a rapid speed, carrying the four Love-Easter's, Marco, Benson and Khan to the Command Station. On the ride, the four Love-Easter replica's grilled Benson about whether or not she had any sisters for them. Typical of the way Marco remembered his friend Dray. He smiled as Benson verbally spared with the Love-Easter duplicates about whether or not she would introduce them to her sisters.

The doors slid open and revealed the rectangular Command Station of the *Amistad*. There were three unconscious Marines on the floor. Marco walked in first an observed that the machinery, computers, fixtures, chairs and other fixtures on the lower level were in pristine condition. The two upper walkways which housed the majority of the computer banks, weapons section command seats and engineering seats were not damaged. The sky roof, with the large see through metal ceiling was not ruptured or cracked.

Other than the three Marines, everyone else in the room seemed fine. The room had each of the sections seats taken. There were several other officers and civilian employees standing and waiting what was going to occur next. Marco noted that many of the attendees had despair on their faces. They looked defeated.

Marco saw the woman he had known as Penelope Smith, who was actually Penelope Rosenburg, standing in the middle of the Command Station. Her long hair was straight and perfect, not one strand disturbed. She had on a one piece, form fitting black leather suit which accentuated her curvaceous body. She had on a pair of white knee high boots, a large black back pack and a laser rifle slung over her right shoulder. She also had a short sword sheathed in a scabbard that hung down the side of her left leg. Marco noticed that the majority of the men were unable to keep their eyes off of the Rosenburg woman.

Next to her was another man that should have been dead, Lieutenant Garrison, the deceased Security Chief of Space Station Cy-7. He was also wearing a black leather one piece suit and black boots. He was laughing as another Drayton Love-Easter clone had told him something that must have been humorous. That made a total of five duplicates of Love-Easter on the Command Station. Marco was getting a headache trying to grasp the reality before him.

Marco noticed that Captain Bruce Allen was sitting in his Captain's chair, his head resting in his hands. He seemed to be ashamed that his ship had been taken over. Captain Allen was in his late fifties and had an eye patch over his left eye, having lost it in a battle against marauding creatures years ago on planet Athena. He had a scar on the left side of his face from the chin to the top of his skull. Although cosmetic surgery would have covered the scar and would have given him a new eye, Allen had refused such offers. He claimed his wounds from the past made him who he was. He had shaved his head bald so that all could see the extent of the large scar. The battles he had participated in on planet Athena had grown into legend. It was written in the history books that the humans and the native aliens lived in some manner of harmony for several generations. Then the rebellion began. The aliens wanted the humans to leave their planet. The Glorious Leader refused and ordered his troops to conquer and subjugate the planet. Allen was a young flight officer at the time and had been stationed as a squadron commander on one of the Athenian moons. Allen led his squadron against the alien

Sajhootai, which was the air force of the native Athenians. Allen and his pilots fought against odds of ten to one and won the day for humanity. He was awarded the Medal of Valor for his bravery in that war. Most of his physical injuries were a reminder that the victory over the Sajhootai came at a price. Allen lost an eye and thousands of humans perished before the aliens surrendered. Captain Allen wore the dark blue uniform of the Space Command pilot corps, which was where he had risen in rank over the years. He had broad shoulders and a thick mustache.

Seated next to the Captain was Admiral of the Second Fleet, Rajesh Khan. The Admiral was about one hundred years old, kept alive by numerous mechanical body parts. He wore the traditional head dress of a Sikh from India and sported a long beard. His uniform was the dark blue ceremonial Class A issue from the pilot corps. Khan had many wives and children. All of his children had joined the military at his direction. Service in the Space Command was a family tradition. Khan was the oldest person on the Command Station. He had grey streaks in his hair and wrinkles around his eyes that seemed dull from decades of warfare. Like Allen, Khan was listed prominently in the history annals that were studied by military cadets over the eight solar systems. He had earned numerous medals from the United Nations Security Council and had three personally given to him by the Glorious Leader. His brothers and sisters had also served in the Space Command and the majority had lost their lives in some of the wars. Only two had been able to retire to live out the remainder of their years. One of them had retired to the moon called Chronos. The Red Javelin attack on that moon and the death of all humans that lived there, weighed heavily on the mind of Admiral Khan.

Marco walked around the crowded command area, holding Benson's hand. They both nodded to one of their ship mates, David "Chirp" Rawlings, who was standing on the rail of the third level, his clawed feet keeping him balanced on the metal beam. Rawlings had been one of the offspring of the genetic experiments on planet Athena. When he was conceived, it had been by in vitro medical procedures. Rawlings mother had allowed the doctors to add to her fertilized eggs DNA splices from Hawks from old Earth. The doctors believed that the children in the test would be born with superior eyesight. They were correct, to an extent. They did all have the ability to see for miles. But they also grew large wings on their backs and had claws for feet and hands. Chirp Rawlings had been born with all of those qualities. With his eyes, he could see farther than any human could with the naked eye. With his wings, he could fly just as any bird from ancient Earth. Rawlings studied at the Academy to become a weapons specialist. When he graduated, he joined the Army ranks and was currently a First Lieutenant.

Marco and Barnes stopped walking around the room when they met their pilot corps commander on the *Amistad*. Commander Dana Del Rey had on her dark blue Class C uniform. She had been a model as a young woman and was still attractive in her forties. Her long dark hair was tied back in a ponytail. She was about five feet tall and known to be a fantastic pilot. She was also a good leader to her pilots and treated everyone under her command even handedly.

Marco heard murmuring from some of the other officers that the invaders were able to take the engineering floor and weapons section with little effort. They forced Captain Allen to surrender by threatening to shut down the life support systems that regenerated the oxygen for the large Battle Cruiser. Had they carried out the threat, it would have meant certain death for the crew members. The Captain had no alternative but to capitulate. Marco heard others speaking of some high ranking officers that had been decapitated by the usurpers.

"Your attention, please!" The Garrison Replicant yelled to quiet the murmur of conversation. The original, or the real Garrison had died a year earlier when Ella Ragnarsson had tampered with his space suit, called an enviro-suit, just before he left his post on Space Station Cy-7 to investigate a tragic explosion of a civilian transport. While out in space recovering evidence, his suit malfunctioned and he died due to lack of oxygen. This specific duplicate was one of the original twenty-five clones of Garrison created by the Rosenburg women. Since the original batch had been created by Penelope's siblings, they had created another one hundred Garrison's. Each of the Garrison clones had agreed to take on different first names, and go by those names only, to help others in telling them apart. He had taken the name of Peter Garrison. "It is time to present to each of you the facts so that you may make an informed decision."

Marco and Benson held each other's hands tighter. Benson felt as if she was cold. She felt dread in listening to the words of these individuals. They had taken over an entire Battle Cruiser and her crew of one thousand five hundred men and women. She wondered how a handful of people could complete such an act.

Penelope Rosenburg stepped forward, smiling at the

assembled officers of the defeated space craft. "Thank you. As you know, my friends and I have executed fifty-one of your officers on all five of your Battle Cruisers. Each death was absolutely necessary."

"My Executive Officer?" Captain Allen interrupted her, his voice loud with anger. "My chief of security? My chief weapons officer? My head of engineering? The other Captains on the other ships? And why kill the other flight officers? What good could come from you cutting off the heads of these people that have been my friends for years?" His voice was grief stricken.

Penelope walked to the Captain and knelt before him. "Look in my eyes, Captain."

Allen slowly lifted his head and looked into the face of the beautiful Rosenburg woman.

"I killed them all precisely because they were never your friends," Penelope nodded as she spoke. She had stressed the word 'never' to drive home the point. "They were all spies, waiting to turn on each and every one of you. They were all united with one thing in common, to protect the Glorious Leader, who was also their grandfather, great grandfather and great great grandfather. They were all Murdock's, Sikorsky's, Welker's, Tsukifuji's, Jenssen's and other last names of the seed of the Sikorsky family. They were on your five Battle Cruisers to kill each one of you if their family determined you should die."

"Aren't the Rosenburg's descendants of the Sikorsky's, too?" Lieutenant Khan spoke up. "If you are one of them, how can we trust you?"

"Good question," Penelope nodded. "Very fair. You are correct, I am one of them. Whether you decide to trust me or not is your choice. I was exposed to some horrific events a year ago. My family consisted of mass murderers, at least one serial rapist and many narcissists. I saw children orphaned, good people were murdered and all the while I was afraid to stand up to my family. I knew their actions were evil. About a year ago, I held a sobbing child in my arms. Her whole family had been wiped out because of my family. As I held that child I made a choice, a final decision. I put aside my fears of dying, my fear of retaliation by my family and I decided that the reign of terror had to end. I have turned on my family to side with the ideals of self-determination and freedom. If we do not act, the Sikorsky family will rule all of the human race for eternity. It ends now. It must."

"You speak of open treason," Del Rey said loudly.

Penelope turned and faced Del Rey, "Yes, that is

what I advocate and I am not alone. You, Commander, will join us today."

Del Rey laughed out loud, "Really? That is quite presumptuous of you."

"Yes, perhaps I am being a bit presumptuous. But I know some things that the rest of you do not. You see, the Sikorsky's will live forever because they each harvest body parts from the young. They use their skin, their eyes, their hearts, their livers, kidneys and other body parts to replace their aging organs. When the Sikorsky family has a person harvested for their internal organs and their skin, they use drugs to keep the victim awake during the extractions. They afford them no pain killers as the Sikorsky's enjoy the cries of agony when the victims are being cut open by the surgeons. I have personally witnessed some of those barbaric procedures. They must be stopped. You had a little sister, Commander Del Rey. Cora was her name? She was one of their victims. The Sikorsky's had her kidnaped with some other young teen age girls and did this to them. Your sister died when they forcibly removed her body parts from her for their own use." Penelope noted the look of shock in Del Rey's eyes.

Del Rey looked away from Penelope. She had not thought of her missing older sister for over a decade. The entire Del Rey family had given up hope of ever finding her. Cora Del Rey had vanished without a trace while vacationing in Belize. Cora had been invited by some of her friends to celebrate a birthday. Five young girls, Cora included, disappeared on that trip. None of the five were ever found. Dana Del Rey had been just six years old when Cora was lost to her family.

Penelope walked over to face the Admiral, "Sir, you lost a brother, six nephews and twenty-three nieces on the moon called Chronos."

"Yes, yes I did," Kahn answered slowly.

"I am deeply sorrowed by your loss, Admiral. The planetacide we all were witnesses to was committed by the Glorious Leader." Penelope said loudly. "Sikorsky must be prosecuted for the murder of those eight hundred thousand souls. Commander Del Rey? Your aunt and uncle were also living on Chronos. The Glorious Leader killed them all."

"We all know that he ordered the attack. He took credit for it in one of his speeches," Khan challenged.

Penelope smiled, "Yes, Admiral, I know. Each of you heard him admit to the massacre himself. He killed all of those people to send a message to all of humanity. But his high ranking children were also involved in the decision to massacre the population of Chronos. Computer, please play the disk, cut seven."

The crowd on the Command Station began whispering as a three dimensional image appeared before them. There was Vladimir Sikorsky, Admiral of the Fleet Sikorsky and Admiral of Scientific Exploration Welker involved in a conversation. The three men admit to knowledge of the launching of an offensive weapon to annihilate the people of Chronos. Many in the top two levels of the Command Station gasped at the admissions being made. The images faded away and the crowd was now shouting at each other. Some yelling was occurring.

Del Rey had tears in her eyes. She had sworn her life, her allegiance to the UN and to the Sikorsky's. She was speechless. All her career had been dedicated to a family that had committed mass murder. They had sliced her older sister up to use her body parts. The obscenity of it all angered Del Rey more than she had ever experienced. For many reasons, she had believed the lie that the Glorious Leader took blame for the deaths on Chronos to cover up for some alien invasion.

"How did you get that recording?" Captain Allen shouted down the others as he stood up pointing his index finger at Penelope. "That must be a fake, a forgery!"

Penelope walked to the Captain and placed her left

hand on his cheek. "My dear Captain. You are the one man that was betrayed by the Sikorsky's worst of all. My heart has always ached for you, for your pain, your guilt. The hole in your soul for what they did to you and your life."

"What are you talking about?" Allen demanded.

"Your fiancé, Iridia." Penelope said with sympathy in her voice. "The Royal Family had her murdered on your wedding day. Computer, play track one."

More three dimensional images appeared of men and women talking. It was Sikorsky, Dell Ragnarsson and Five Star General of the Army, Dean Murdock.

"We cannot allow the Allen's and the Fenster's to be united in marriage," Murdock was saying. "Dell, we brought you in to assist us with this problem. What do you suggest?"

"Naturally you cannot allow the union to occur. Those two families together would have the potential to rival the Royal Family in monies and weaponry." A younger Dell Ragnarsson had said. "I will cut the woman up on her wedding day. Her body will be found by the wedding guests. As we all know, the first suspect in a brutal murder is always the spouse or significant other. The Fenster's will cast blame on the Allen's, even without proof. It will cast a shadow over both families for generations to come. They will never be able to cooperate with one another and therefore the power of the Royal Family will go on. How does that sound?"

The Glorious Leader clapped his hands together. "Bravo. Do it. Kill the bitch."

The image faded from view to reveal Captain Allen on his knees, weeping like a child. Allen had, at one time in his life, been absolutely loyal to his grandfather. Allen had been directed by his elders to marry a woman from the Fenster family. His bride to be was Iridia Fenster. He agreed to marry the woman out of his sense of obligation to the family. About a month before the wedding, Iridia had found a way to secretly meet Bruce Allen. She wanted to get to know her future husband. The two found they were attracted to one another and had many similar interests. They began meeting behind the backs of their family and in a short amount of time, they became lovers. Their wedding day came and Allen was the happiest man alive. He had fallen in love with Iridia. Their marriage was no longer one out of duty to family. They were in love. Before they could conduct the ceremony and say their vows to one another, someone had found Iridia at the church and stabbed her to death. Her bloody corpse was discovered by her father. The Fenster's blamed Bruce Allen for killing Iridia, believing that he had not really wanted to go through with the wedding. He protested his innocence. The murder of Iridia created a massive void between the Allen's and Fenster's. He lost the love of his life and left Earth as an accused murderer. Since there was no DNA or eye witness evidence to tie him to the murder, he was never charged with the crime. But the shroud of guilt brought by the accusations followed Bruce Allen for the remainder of his life.

"How dare you show that? Where did you obtain such footage?" Allen demanded. "Who was he? The man that killed Iridia?"

"I am so sorry, Captain," Penelope said softly. "I have connections. Everything at the Tower of the Glorious Leader is taped. As a family member I can access the information. The man that murdered Iridia was a sicario, or an assassin, named Dell Ragnarsson. He is a very dangerous man and he worked for the Sikorsky's and Rosenburg's for the last two decades. He and his family of assassins have killed thousands. He recently was involved in the Blood Moon Incident as one of the organizers of the ambush on the cadets. We believe he is dead, vaporized on the Blood Moon in a Raumschiff explosion caused by a collision in mid-air." She put a sympathetic hand on Allen's shoulder. "You loved Iridia, more than anyone could know."

"Yes."

"And they killed her, to keep your family separated from the Fenster's. That is how the Sikorsky mind works." Penelope turned her attention to Marco. "You also have been targeted by the Royal Family."

Marco held up his hand at her. He knew she was going to bring up his aunt and uncle, the Spinelli's. He had no desire for his family tragedy to be aired to the crowded Command Station. "Stop it! Yes, my aunt, uncle and my cousins were murdered by the Sikorsky's. I already know. Everyone here knows about what happened to me on the Blood Moon. Please stop embarrassing us with our pasts. This is not healthy for any of us. Why don't you just cut to the chase and tell us what your demands are?"

Penelope nodded. She saw that Del Rey, Khan and Allen were all three showing open emotions before the others. "Very well. I will stop. The question now is simple. In or out? I intend to destroy my family and their two hundred year rule. Who is with me?"

There was silence on the Command Station for many minutes. Finally, Captain Allen stood to his feet, wiping wet tears from his cheek. "I am with you. Iridia was beautiful, sweet, caring and kind. They butchered her. For

Iridia, I am with you."

Admiral Khan stood from his chair and walked over next to Allen. Khan had no love for the Sikorsky family. He had always questioned their refusal to allow free elections so that men and women could vote their conscience and choose their leaders. Khan had also participated in many battles against alien races that had been peaceful. By orders of the Glorious Leader, those races had been wiped out. Khan realized that he had much in common with Penelope in that he had also been too scared to stand up to the Sikorsky's. Now he had his chance to try and set things right. "Count me in. Humanity deserves to have freedom from tyranny such as this. I will fight for liberty for the people."

Del Rey nodded in agreement. Many other officers began to verbally assent to joining the Rebellion.

Marco looked into Benson's eyes. She was crying as she recalled her classmates that had lost their lives on the Blood Moon. Two of the victims had been her best friends. "They killed Torch and Nick on the Blood Moon."

"And Pierre and Porfirio," Marco wiped the tears from her eyes. "We are probably all going to die if we fight the power and technology of the Glorious Leader."

"My love, we are already on borrowed time."

Benson smiled. "We should have died on that Blood Moon with the others. It is only by the grace of the Gods that we are still here. We may as well be useful with our borrowed time and die as traitors fighting for liberty."

Marco held Benson in his arms, "My brother Dominic and all of our friends will become our enemies if we do this. If civil war is what is going to happen, how do we fight our own siblings and friends?"

Benson shook her head, "Don't worry about those things, Marco. Your brother is smart. Dominic will make the right choice when it is placed in his path. Hopefully he will understand that we are doing this for him."

Marco turned to face Penelope. Everyone had eyes on Benson and Marco. They were the only two that had not made a decision.

"Ellen and I will fight against tyranny," Marco stated loudly. "We are with you."

Captain Allen stood next to Penelope and looked over to his young communications officer on the second level of the Command Station. "Lieutenant Gee, patch me into the ships. I need to address all of the crews."

"I'll speak first," Admiral Khan informed them.

Gee, as a hybrid human and Akarzdamedian, was eight feet tall and lanky with long arms. He began pressing some buttons on her control panel and looked down to his Captain, "You are on, sir."

"Ladies and gentlemen, please give me your attention. This is your Admiral speaking. Just a century ago, Admiral Un orchestrated an attempted coup against the Royal Family. She commanded a flight group of seven older design battle ships and she led them into war just outside of the orbit of Planet New Quebec. The Glorious

Leader refused to cede power to Un and his family met her in battle. Admiral Un failed and she died in the battle along with the majority of her co-conspirators. Some of their space suit encased bodies are still floating among the wreckage of the ships that were destroyed in that war. The Royals will sometimes show footage of that outer space graveyard as a warning to others to avoid challenging them. Now, I never knew Un. I wasn't even born when that battle occurred. But her attempt is inspirational in what we must do together.

"For decades I have served in the Space Command. I worked my way up from the rank of Ensign to where I am today. When I was first promoted to a Captain of a Battle Cruiser, I became a member of an elite fraternity of officers. Very few of us ever ascend to that rank or position. I was honored and proud, yet humbled at the same time. It was a great responsibility to hold the rank of Captain and an even greater one to be an Admiral. But I speak to you today as a man that has failed you all. Not only have I failed you, but I have failed humanity. You see, many Captains and Admirals that pay attention to the political scene know that our leaders are not mentally well. They are inept at times, despicable at best and commit acts of abject cruelty at their worst. Most of the Admiralty that learns of the atrocities of the Glorious Leader turn a blind eye to it. You see, it was due to something that was never spoken. It was because of that fear that was a whisper in the wind, that if one spoke out in dissent, then their life would be forfeit. So, those of us in power that could have actually attempted to end the sadistic rule of the Sikorsky's never acted. We stood by in silence while innocents suffered and died. We allowed the barbaric behavior to be repeated over and over again by our omission. We practiced a doctrine of avoidance, pretending that the issues regarding the Royal Family did not exist and as we did so, people died. But today, those of us that can make a difference need to stand together and end the dictatorship of the Sikorsky regime. I speak to you as a man that is saddened by his lack of action in the past because I know my unwillingness to act has caused others to suffer. I will no longer stand by and do nothing. I hope that all of you will follow me to finally bring hope and freedom to the people. I plan on telling all of humanity that the time has come to no longer hide in the shadows afraid of the MI soldiers that might arrest them. It is time to fight. I now ask that Captain Allen address you."

"This is the Captain," Allen began. "As you all know, we were boarded two hours ago and we were forced to surrender. The other four ships of our fleet have also ceased hostilities. I am going to confer with Admiral Khan regarding many issues, chief among them will be reorganizing the crews of the five fleets. We have many open slots to fill in the section commanders positions. Many of you will receive field promotions. I ask that each of you remain calm as this transition period continues. We are safe for now. Your families are not in harm's way. Remain calm and await further instructions. Captain Allen, out."

Gee cut the open ship wide broadcast.

Allen turned to the Admiral, "We need new Captain's for the other four Battle Cruisers. Commander Del Rey, I think would be an excellent choice."

"Yes, she would," the Admiral agreed. "Commander Del Rey, you are hereby promoted to Captain and will assume the duties as commander of the Rorke's Drift. I will take over command of the Montenegro. I will instruct the security chief of the Nigeria, Lieutenant Commander Gloria Harvard, to take command of that vessel. The New Delhi will be captained by Lieutenant Talisia Rogers from the pilot corps."

Allen faced Penelope, "Okay, lady. You have yourself an army, air force and marines. What would you have us do?"

"We are going to quarantine Sikorsky's Planet so no more of those weapons of mass destruction can be launched." Penelope said simply. "We cannot allow another Chronos disaster to occur. I will be coordinating with the other Fleet that has already joined us so that we can begin plans to attack."

"Which other Fleet is with us?" Admiral Khan asked.

"Admiral Cardenas is on our side and invading planet Cootron as we speak," Penelope stated softly to the two men. "And in a few weeks we hope to add Admiral Weems."

Khan and Allen smiled at that. Cardenas was an excellent military strategist, as was Weems. With three Fleets of Battle Cruisers together, the little insurrection they had joined may stand a chance of success.

"When can we expect them to join us at Sikorsky's Planet?" Khan asked her.

"I anticipate that they will be ready in about two to three weeks. While you will be ensuring the safety of humanity by blocking those Red Javelin's, Admiral Cardenas will be invading planet Cootron and freeing the people there," Penelope whispered to Khan and Allen. Even though all of the officers assented to joining the rebellion, she was cognizant of the reality that some men and women would attempt to use the situation as a chance to advance or to be paid. That desire could lead to loose lips and she did not want the main plans of revolution to reach the ears of the Glorious Leader.

CHAPTER FOUR

Newly promoted Captain Dana Del Rey walked onto the rectangular shaped Command Station of the United Nations Space Command Battle Cruiser *Rorke's Drift*.   She noticed that the blood stained floor and walls had been washed clean. Just a day earlier the floors were covered in Royal Family blood from the decapitations performed by Penelope Rosenburg and her fellow conspirators. Del Rey noticed that there were four female Marines at the two elevator entrances with laser rifles in their hands. The Captain's chair was empty as was the seats for the Executive Officer, pilot, astral navigator and security. There were several junior officers standing at attention for her as she slowly approached the chair in the center of the room.

Del Rey had dreamed of the day she would be the Captain of her own Battle Cruiser. She had never imagined she would be the Captain of a ship full of insurrection minded crew members. Del Rey sat in the chair and motioned for the rest of the crew to sit down. The junior officers looked suspiciously at the five men that had accompanied her into the Command Station. Del Rey had been given three Drayton Love Easter Replicants and two Frank Garrison's. The five duplicates were gifts from Penelope Rosenburg to assist in the staffing of the large Battle Cruiser. All five were wearing black outfits with black boots and had several weapons attached to their web belts.

Del Rey had learned that the Garrisons had chosen the names Lazarus and Tucson. The three Love-Easter Replicants were happy to go by their initials and numbers. Del Rey learned to call them DLE 211, DLE 212 and DLE 213. She wondered how the clones could interact with one another so easily. They had the same physical features, same faces and same memories. Del Rey wondered how the duplication process had become possible. She had heard of scientists attempting the science of copying a life form. It had been done before, but not like this. Not to this level of excellence. Each of the Love-Easter clones looked exactly the same in every detail. The same was true for the Garrison copies. They each acted like real humans. Had Del Rey not been told that they were clones, she would never had been able to tell.

Many of the junior officers and the enlisted Marines had looks of hope in their eyes. Some had fear and uncertainty on their faces. Del Rey smiled at each of the crew members and cleared her throat.

"I was told that each of you agreed with the Rosenburg woman and renounced the Glorious Leader," Del Rey began as she made eye contact with each and every crew member. "As you all know, I was serving as one of the top pilots under Captain Allen on the Amistad. He and Admiral Khan promoted me to be the Captain of your ship."

Del Rey paused for a moment and then stood back up and walked around each of her crew. "That is right. This is your ship. Not mine. I am open to suggestions and criticism. I want all of you to feel free to tender your advice to me."

Del Rey motioned toward the Love-Easter and Garrison Replicants. "Do not be alarmed by these five men. They were sent to assist in the running of the ship while we make way for our primary mission."

First Lieutenant Dia Cho was standing on the second level of the tri-level Command Station and was leaning over the safety rails listening to her new Captain speak. Cho and her wife, Felicia Essex, had been assigned to the *Rorke's Drift* four years earlier when they had graduated from the Clovis Academy. Both of the women were assigned to the Weapons Section and had recently been promoted from Second Lieutenant to First Lieutenant. Cho and Essex had been raising their four children on the Battle Cruiser as they worked hard at building their careers. Cho noticed the three clones of her old friend, Drayton Love-Easter, and her eyes widened with surprise.

"Dray!" Cho yelled out with glee. She ran for the ladders and slid down them. The three Love-Easters realized who she was and they ran to her. The rest of the crew watched the four hug one another for a few moments.

"Dia! We did not know you were on this ship!" DLE211 said with joy.

"Is Felicia on board? How are the children?" DLE213 asked.

"Yes, she is here." Cho answered each of the clones. "The children are just fine. They are getting bigger. How? How are there three of you? Felicia and I cried our hearts out when we thought you were dead."

DLE212 took her hand in his, "Dia, we were dead. Or our host, the real Drayton, was dead. The Rosenburg family caused his death. We are clones of the original Dray. We have his DNA and all of his memories and experiences in our cloned brains. We are him in every respect."

Cho hugged the three clones to her. Although she only had the privilege of spending one year with Love-Easter at the Academy, she had a close bond to him. She had liked his mind, the way that he saw the world and interpreted events. He was different, possibly the result from being the son of a minister. "Then I love all three of you, just as I did the original. When we have time, Felicia would love to see you again. I want you to meet our children. You would all love them."

Del Rey cleared her throat. She had several orders to give out and arrangements to make. She had been instructed by Admiral Khan to field promote several of the *Rorke's Drift* officers to fill the vacant command team positions. She looked over the assembled crew members and her gaze settled on Lieutenant Cho.

"Lieutenant, you serve in the weapons section?" Del Rey asked her.

"Yes, ma'am." Cho answered.

"Who is your commanding officer?"

Cho looked at the other crew members and back at her new Captain. "She was killed as was our executive officer."

Del Rey pursed her lips for a second and nodded,

"So I take it all of the remaining Weapons officers are First Lieutenant or lower in rank?"

Cho nodded, "Yes, ma'am."

Del Rey smiled at Cho, "Well, it would seem that Drayton vouches for you. You are promoted to Captain of the Weapons Section."

Cho's eyes widened, "Me? But some of the others might be better qualified."

"Captain Cho, you are now my weapons chief," Del Rey dismissed her protests. "Select your second in command of that section on your own and let me know of your selection. I will assign DLE211 and DLE212 to work with you. I need the weapons section operating at full capacity. We will be expecting action very soon."

"Yes ma'am," Cho nodded. She began to realize the seriousness of the moment. She was put in charge of all of the battle ready capabilities of the Battle Cruiser. "Where are we attacking first?"

Del Rey shook her head and continued looking over the junior officers as she attempted to size them up. "No, we will not be attacking. Not yet. Tentatively, our first mission will be initiating a blockade around Sikorsky's Planet."

"Which we are certain will draw out the First Fleet

under Admiral Perdiccas," Tucson Garrison added. Based on the recommendation of Penelope Rosenburg, Del Rey had selected Tucson as her chief tactician. "And that will be when there will be a battle."

One of the pilots that was present, Lieutenant Targa Jara White raised her hand. She waited until Del Rey pointed to her. "Captain, many of us have families on board. If we put a blockade around the home planet of the Glorious Leader, then we will be in harm's way. What about our children and spouses?"

Del Rey smiled at her. White had been a reliable squadron leader and a talented pilot. Del Rey had interacted with White socially and professionally over the past two years. She found White to be a talented pilot and learned that she had been a promising cadet at Newton Academy. White served with distinction on every assignment. White had also married a computer technician named Sylvester White and they had two children. Del Rey needed to field promote one of her squadron commanders to take command of the pilots. White was a good choice.

"Lieutenant White, you are now my commander of the pilots section. No worry about your families as the Admiral has contacted a few groups friendly to our cause. We will stop at some safe location on the way to Sikorsky's

Planet and all non-combatants will be left there. There are several planets and moons full of citizens that have moved to overthrow the Royal Family and their leadership. Any one of those places will protect our children and nonmilitary spouses until we return."

White smiled slightly at the answer and her field promotion. She was relieved that her husband and children would be removed from harm's way. Due to her duties as a squadron commander, her husband had taken on the majority of the child rearing duties. While White would spend her time on deep space patrol or training sessions with her squadron, her husband would be the one to feed, bathe and take care of their precious offspring. "Thank you ma'am."

"Now, Commander White, would you kindly make best speed to the edge of the Sikorsky Solar System? We have a blockade to begin."

White sat down in the pilot's seat and began initiating the flight plan. One of the Garrison Replicants sat down next to her in the astral navigation seat. He introduced himself as Lazarus Garrison and quickly began typing on his three dimensional computer pad before him. White smiled at the man named Lazarus and the two began to guide the massive Battle Cruiser called *Rorke's Drift* toward the moon called Robert Andrews.

In the weapons section of the *Rorke's Drift* the soldiers and technicians were fast at work loading armor piercing missiles into the launch silos. Supervising the work was Felicia Essex. Her wife, Dia Cho, was spending her time making sure that freshly charged laser batteries were installed in each of the laser canons. They were leaving nothing to chance. During battle, reloading was the most time consuming part for any weapons section operative. Cho and Essex wanted to start off with all rocket silos and laser batteries full to capacity so that reloading would not be an immediate issue in the upcoming space attack.

Tucson Garrison was there helping out the technicians. Cho noticed that the clone had gravitated toward Technical Sergeant Carria Woods. They had been working together, calibrating her computerized targeting mechanism on one of the large laser canons. At one point, Cho though she saw them flirting. Cho wondered if the Garrison clone that called himself Tucson could perform sexually as a normal man could. From the body language and laughter coming from Woods, it was apparent the weapons technician was hoping to find out.

Woods asked Tucson Garrison to meet her at her

quarters after their shift ended. He agreed. Tucson was curious to see if he was able to make love to a woman. He had the real Garrison's memories and experiences in his brain. He recalled the sensation of holding a woman, touching her, kissing her and making love. He wanted to see if it was possible for him as a DNA duplicate to have the same sensations as a normal man.

After his shift ended, Tucson Garrison wasted no time. He walked quickly to the third level of the ship and followed the hallways to the non-commissioned officer's rooms. He located the room number that Woods had told him she would be at. He rang her bell and waited. The door slid open and he was happy to see that Woods was there, waiting for him. She was wearing a red sleeveless half shirt and white panties.

"Come in. A girl could catch a cold if you leave the door open," Woods told him.

Tucson walked in and smiled as she immediately embraced him. They shared a long, lingering kiss. He ran his hands over her body and she began massaging him between the legs. Within seconds Woods and Tucson realized that the cloned body was fully functional. They made love on her floor as if it were their last day of life.

On the Command Station of the Battle Cruiser

Amistad, Captain Bruce Allen had already field promoted crew members to fill the positions left open by the assassinations perpetrated by Penelope Rosenburg. The woman had left as quickly as she had arrived. She left behind the Replicants of Drayton Love Easter that all went by their numbers DLE8, DLE9, DLE10, DLE11 and DLE12. The five Love-Easter Replicants were working in the weapons section and security. The Replicant named Frank Garrison was promoted to security chief of the *Amistad*.

Allen looked over at his two young pilots on the command station. Marco Andolini and Ellen Benson sat next to one another in the pilot seat and astral navigation seat respectively. The two young pilots demonstrated much talent and potential. Allen had determined that the two pilots would be placed in command of two of his flight squadrons when the time came to organize the blockade flights around Sikorsky's Planet. Both Marco and Benson had demonstrated a never say die attitude while on the Blood Moon together. Allen hoped that they both still had some of that fire in their bellies.

Captain Allen had given Penelope two of his crew members to assist her in what she referred to as a covert attack on Sikorsky's Planet. First Lieutenant Shinghi Khan and First Lieutenant David "Chirp" Rawlings left with the woman that was leading the insurrection against the Glorious Leader. She would not tell Allen or Admiral Khan where they were going to attack. She only told them that her mission was one of life and death for billions of lives.

On board her Super Raumschiff, Penelope looked over her command area. In the upper pilots section were clones of Garrison and Love-Easter. Sitting before her were Shinghi Khan, David Rawlings, several duplicates of Garrison, Love-Easter, Ella Ragnarsson (with the memories and experiences of Penelope imprinted in the cloned brain), and clones of Nicolette Rosenburg.

Penelope waited until they were approaching light speed before she addressed the crew. "We are going to attempt to stop any further mass murder."

"How are we going to do that?" Khan had his arms crossed over his chest. He was still wearing his torn black uniform.

Penelope smiled at him, "There is a place where weapons of mass destruction are created. We will invade that facility. But before we do so, we need to recruit more allies."

"So where are we going?" Rawlings shrugged.

"We are going to meet up with Admiral

Yamamoto," Penelope told them. "We have to convince him to join us."

CHAPTER FIVE

Admiral Rajesh Khan had taken in many wives in his lifetime. The majority of them had been by arranged marriage. His parents had accepted dowry payments from other families in return for the privilege of having their daughters married off to the young officer. After Khan left India to attend the Academy, he found other women without the assistance of his parents and married them. He ended up with a dozen wives and the number of children he produced were numerous. Some of his children had followed his example and sought acceptance in one of the many military academies so that they could serve humanity in the Space Command. Others took another direction in their lives and worked in the civilian sector.

Khan had wanted to rid the eight solar systems of Vladimir Sikorsky and his draconian rule years ago. His problem was that had he ever voiced his treasonous thoughts, the Militzia would have arrested him and his life would have ended after a swift trial without the legal benefit of confrontation of the witnesses against him. He would have been disgraced, executed and then the Sikorsky family would have trumped up charges against his children and killed them, too. He did not mind dying, but the knowledge that his government would kill all of his children stayed his hand and Khan never acted on his desires to usher in a new government.

But now it was different. Penelope Rosenburg was a member of the family that Khan had grown to despise. She had determined, as he had, that the people deserved a better leader and a more just legal system. She had inspired Khan to act now and gave him hope that they could bring true freedom to the people of the eight solar systems.

Khan had many problems to take care of before he declared his intentions to the Royal Family. Once he demanded that they surrender to him, they would want to fight. He hoped that they would see that fighting would only cause unnecessary bloodshed and they would be willing to negotiate. But if confrontation did occur, Khan had to make certain that all of the non-military personnel on his five Battle Cruisers were left behind on a safe location.

Khan asked his oldest wife, Charsa, to assist him in solving that dilemma. Charsa Khan had married Rajesh when she was just seventeen years old. She had come from a poor family in southern India of old Earth.   Her father had been a laborer for the Khan family and respected them. He was the one to approach the parents of Rajesh Khan and offer the dowry for marriage. The price was steep and Charsa's family sold all that they owned to buy her a husband.   Charsa felt that the wedding was her duty and never complained before or after. As time passed, she grew to love Rajesh. He had given her a good life. He was kind to her, loving and even encouraged her to study as he served as a pilot in the Space Command.   She gave him several children and held a special place with him as his first wife. Even though he produced many children with his other wives, Charsa was confident that he loved her above the others. She was the one that traveled with him. She was the only one he ever confided in and she was the one that he slept with.   The other wives were there for sexual pleasures and producing children. Charsa performed that for him as well, but she was the one he always stayed with. Over the years, Charsa studied to obtain a degree in physics. She did so using the vast computer memory banks that were sanctioned by some of the best universities in the eight solar systems. She then achieved a Master's Degree in mathematics. She became a Doctorate graduate in Astrophysics at the age of twenty-seven. As such, she served dual roles for Admiral Khan. She served as his First Wife, mother to many of his children, sexual partner and his top scientific advisor.

Rajesh Khan called upon Charsa to assist him in finding the best location to leave the non-combatants on the Second Fleet behind. They were in the Admiral Quarters which consisted of two bathrooms, one shower, a large bedroom, a meeting area, a conference room and a kitchen. They worked in the meeting area to solve the problem. Together, they charted the route from the current location of the Second Fleet to Sikorsky's Planet. They analyzed all of the moons and planets that they would pass by in their flight to that ultimate destination. Charsa concluded and recommended to her husband that all of the children and non-military crew members should be left on the moon called Robert Andrews.

The moon she spoke of was located just outside the solar system of the binary suns that heated Sikorsky's Planet.   The population there had already declared for independence against Sikorsky and was therefore a safe haven for the family members of the Second Fleet. Her husband agreed with her assessment.

"We can leave our younger children there as well as

your sister wives," he said as he looked at the three dimensional chart of the solar system of Sikorsky's Planet. "They should all be safe there. My love, I wish for you to remain there as well."

Charsa met his eyes with unblinking eyes. "Husband, my place is by your side. You have always consulted me on major decisions. You may need my education when you engage the enemy. Certainly we leave all of the children and the other wives behind for their own safety, but I cannot leave your side. It is not in my DNA to do so."

Rajesh nodded as she spoke. He had expected her to refuse. "Charsa, I need for you to hold the family together while I engage the enemy. None of the others can do it. You were the only one that ever showed ambition. You spent all those countless hours studying to become the grand woman you are today. You are the only one I can trust to protect the children. I value your counsel greatly. But this time the children will need you more. You are the First Wife. That means it is your duty to command the family in my absence."

"The Second Wife could act in my place."

"Khadira is beautiful and has produced fine children for us. But she is nowhere near your level of intelligence.

It must be you to lead when I depart for war."

Charsa Khan was silent for several moments. She knew that he was correct. The other sister wives never took the time to try and better themselves. They had all been content to be a wife for the Admiral and nothing more. Some of the wives even criticized Charsa for staying up late to study. They were good mothers, but not one of them possessed leadership abilities. "Very well, my love. I will command the family while you are away."

Rajesh embraced her in his arms and held her close to him. "I love you more than life itself. I never imagined that after thirty-four years of marriage I would love you more today than the first time I realized I had feelings for you."

"And I love you. I only request one thing."

"And what is that?"

"Please return to us alive," Charsa said softly.

"I have no plans to die out there. This will be a turning point for man and woman. Our children will grow up under a new form of government, it will be a fresh start for one and all. We will bring peace back to all of the people." Rajesh whispered the words into her ear.

Charsa looked up into his eyes and softly kissed his lips. "I know you must meet your commanders soon to prepare your course of action. I have one request before you leave."

"And that is?"

"Make love to me."

Rajesh Khan lifted her into his arms and kissed her. He continued kissing her as he carried her to his bedroom.

Captain Bruce Allen had excused himself from the Command Station of the Amistad and left the clone that called himself Frank Garrison in temporary command of the ship. Allen had some personal matters to take care of before they entered any form of combat situation. He walked into his living quarters, which were about the same size as Khan's, and began pulling out some items from a large roll top desk in his meeting room. Allen had accumulated artifacts from many worlds over the years he served in the Space Command. He always sent gifts out to his nieces and nephews, sometimes months in advance, to ensure they would arrive in time for their individual birthdays. He had glowing rocks from New Sao Paolo, swords that had been forged by the alien race on New Quebec, fossils of ancient extinct species from other planets and other forms of weaponry.

Allen began to package up all of the items into boxes so that they could be shipped off to old Earth and reach all of his family. Allen never married after he lost Iridia. He never found love again. He did have a short relationship with a pilot he served with years ago. She had been married to another man and that other man had been Allen's close friend and a fellow pilot. He and his wife separated for a short time when he was sent on a ship called *Bismark* to go to another world. The *Bismark* disappeared and was never heard from again. With the man missing in action, Allen had an affair with his wife. She gave birth to his son.

To Allen's chagrin, the woman did not give the child the surname of Allen. She named the child after her missing husband. Allen was hurt by that action and refused to hear out her explanations. He felt his child should bear his name. The difference between them on that issue created an irreparable rift. She went her way and Allen went on with his life without her and his son. The *Bismark* had never been heard from again.

That had been many years ago. There had been many instances when Allen sought to reach out to the mother of his child, not for the purpose of rekindling the romance, but to see how his son had been faring. Each time he considered the notion he would quickly dismiss it.

Now Allen was faced with the fact that death could

be imminent.   He wanted his son to have all of his cherished belongings. When the *Amistad* arrived at the location selected by the Admiral to drop off the non-military crew members, Allen would have the items shipped to his son from there. He picked up a large broad sword that had been the weapon of choice used by the large gorilla looking aliens on New Moscow. Allen was a man that kept himself in shape with regular trips to the gymnasium. But even he had difficulty lifting the heavy weapon with both hands. He recalled how the giant creatures fought in battle. They were fierce, strong, fast on their feet and would not surrender.

Now most of them were dead. The superior firepower of the humans wiped them out. Allen had been there as a chief pilot on another Battle Cruiser. He had flown an Allen Fighter ship on several strafing runs and vaporized thousands of the New Moscow aliens. He did it all for the glory of humanity and Vladimir Sikorsky. Allen recalled that he felt a strong level of guilt as he helped kill the aliens. All they had wanted was to live.

Humanity wanted them to die and humanity won.

Allen hoped that his son would be able to appreciate all of the items. He wondered if his mother ever revealed the truth about his lineage. Most likely she had not as she had been ashamed of the fact that she was disloyal to her husband. She had demanded that he never reveal the truth to the young boy and Allen promised her he would not. That had been almost fifteen years ago. He had never heard from her again.

Allen hoped beyond hope that Khan would have a laser proof plan in place to force Sikorsky to cede his power over and avoid a war. Allen had grown to care for all of his crew members and wanted each of them to live long and fruitful lives. They were all good men and women, hardworking and dedicated. Above all else, they had been loyal to Allen over the years, especially his pilot corps.

Allen spent several hours boxing up the prized items for shipment. Once he finished that task, he began to contemplate what he would do with his money. As an Allen, he was a millionaire several times over. He was a frugal man and never spent when he did not need to. He had given much thought as to the fate of his fortune if he died in the coming war. Allen found a bourbon bottle that was half full and opened it. He took a large drink before he started.

"Computer, begin recording my last will and testament." Allen spoke up.

"Ready," the computer voice had no emotion.

"I grant my two hundred thirty-seven thousand shares of stock in the Allen Corporation to my niece, Christian Allen. If she pre-deceases me, then I order that those shares of stock go to her sister, Angelica. Upon my death, I ask that my monies be divided as follows. One hundred million Empire dollars to be given to the Newark Orphanage to be dispersed for the benefit of the children living there. One hundred million dollars to be given to a scholarship fund in my name to Fordham University. I ask that the Board of Regents divide the monies up into scholarship awards to pay full tuition and books to under-privileged students that attend. One hundred million dollars to the terra forming department of Oklahoma State University. One hundred million dollars to the Mars University of Under Water Farming Technology. I give one hundred million dollars to the Varitackia Research Institute located on Copper City, Mars. And I give all of my remaining money to Andrea Phillips Seward for her use in any way she sees fit. After her passing, I want the remainder of those sums to go to her son, Terrance Seward. End recording."

"Should I send this to your lawyers?" the computer asked.

"Yes," Allen said and took another drink of bourbon.   His personal affairs were finished. He was now prepared to fight and die if need be. He walked to his bathroom, brushed his teeth to eliminate the odor of bourbon from his breath, smoothed out his uniform with his hands and then left his quarters to return to duty.

In the docking bay of the *Amistad*, just under eight hundred pilots were checking on the small Allen Fighter Type ships and battle ready Raumschiffs. Lieutenant Junior Grade Ezra Tulley was sitting in her seat aboard her Allen Fighter ship. A recent graduate from Achilles Academy, she was just twenty-two years old and terrified of the fact that her shipmates were all hell-bent on committing treason. Tulley noticed that some of the other pilots in her squadron were acting as if they did not have a care in the world. She saw Lieutenant Patricia Dwyer kissing her boyfriend as she was being pressed up against the far hull of the docking area. Tulley was not a voyeur but could not help but notice as Dwyer allowed the man to begin feel her out in front of everyone present. Some of the pilots were cheering them on.

Tulley heard a rapping sound on her hull. She looked away from the public display of Dwyer and her boyfriend to look at whoever it was that was hitting her hull. She smiled when she saw Marco Andolini waiving at her.

"You okay Tulley?" Marco asked.

"I think so. I'm a little scared," she admitted. Marco was the star of their squadron of forty-two ships. Everyone knew him from the Blood Moon and had witnessed his heroics. He was friendly to all of the other pilots and was hugging everyone when he would see them. Tulley liked him, especially his positive outlook on everything.

"We're all scared. You would not be human if you were not.   Fear is healthy in combat. It will keep your senses sharp and help keep you alive." Marco told her. "I hear that Captain Allen will be making an announcement to us all in a few hours. I think that he is going to let us know what our plans are."

"Do you think that the Sikorsky's will surrender without a fight?" Tulley asked him hopefully.

"No. I think that they will need to be forced," he responded. He could hear people against the far hull shouting and cheering. "What the heck is going on over there?"

"Patricia is having sex with her weapons section boyfriend," Tulley informed him after she glanced back over at the hull to see Dwyer on her back being mounted in front of the growing crowd of cheering pilots.

Marco laughed and waived at Tulley as he ran to his own ship. He climbed up the hand holds on the side and leaped into his padded seat. He began his security checks and did his best to ignore the cheers over Dwyer's obscene public performance. He liked Tulley, she was a good girl and a better pilot than she gave herself credit for. He hoped that she had the stomach for a dog fight in deep space.

Captain Allen came on the ship wide broadcast system. He first called for everyone's attention. Marco stopped what he was doing to hear out his Captain. Tulley was looking up at the high ceiling of the docking area as if she were looking for the person speaking.

Marco noticed that some of the other pilots in his squadron were playing dice against the west side of the hull.   Roberta Largo, Mary Winston, Zalia Jeong and Azalia Dell were taking turns tossing dice against the wall and betting money between each throw. As he watched them, Marco wondered what type of currency or money transactions would exist under a new form of government. Would paper money be replaced making gambling on dice games or poker obsolete? He hoped not as he had been a decent poker player at the Academy. For some reason, most of his crew members did not play cards but spent their time rolling dice instead.

Marco watched the four rolling dice. They were all good pilots and decent ladies to associate with. He and Benson had befriended them and they would associate with one another from time to time. Largo had gone to Achilles Academy and came from a family of farmers. Winston was from planet Athena and her mother had been a reporter and was a single mother. Dell was quiet about her background. She was the one that would generally buy the first round of drinks when they would gather at Take Ten. Jeong was from a small school on Mars called Broussard Academy. Her parents were engineers that had helped with the building of dams on the Martian surface to maintain the manmade rivers on the planet surface. Dwyer, who was giving the others a live pornographic show, had been an orphan and signed up for the Academy at the age of seventeen to escape the strict rules of her placement.

He focused in on the words of Captain Allen.

"We will be making a slight detour on the way to Sikorsky's Planet," Allen's voice informed them. "Admiral Khan wanted me to address you and give you this final offer. We do not want any of you feel like you must join this mission. If you do not want to be involved, we will stop on the lunar body called Robert Andrews which is in the far reaches of the Sikorsky Solar System. We will be having all civilian crew members and children transported to the surface of Robert Andrews and left there for their own safety. I want all non-military personnel to pack all of your personal belongings and be prepared to leave the ship in twelve hours. All children will be transported along with you. If you are a parent, we encourage you to stay with your children. There is no shame in staying behind. No one will judge you at all. Thank you all for having been a wonderful crew. I will forever be grateful to you all for you service."

The broadcast when silent.

Marco noticed that Dell was throwing the dice as if she had not heard any speeches. Marco went about finishing his security checks in his small ship. He knew that Benson was several bays down to his east, checking her ship. He silently prayed that they would both get through the conflict alive.

Commander Del Rey made a similar announcement to her crew on the *Rorke's Drift*. Technical Sergeant Carria Woods was in the weapons section, setting the calibrations on some of the other laser canons in the weapons section as she listened to Del Rey's speech. She smiled in the direction of Dia Cho who gave her a thumbs up. Cho and her wife, Felicia Essex, had discussed the issue of their children being in the middle of a war. Due to their respect for Khan, they had anticipated such an announcement and had already packed all of the belongings of their four children. One of their weapons technicians, Jiannaha Jordan, had three children on board as well. Jordan's husband was going to leave the ship and take their three children and he had volunteered to protect Cho and Essex children until they returned.

Tucson Garrison was lending a hand and Cho found that his knowledge of military tactics and weaponry to be very helpful. Cho also found it interesting that the clone seemed to be extremely affectionate toward Carria Woods. Cho found it interesting that Woods was in good spirits and smiling at Tucson often. Based on their body language, Cho deduced that they had already slept together and had made some agreements regarding a continuing relationship. Cho smiled to herself as Tucson took Woods by the arm and helped her step down from one of the laser canons. Cho wondered if a clone could love. By the way Tucson Garrison was behaving, Cho thought that it was possible.

Admiral Khan, Professor Charsa Khan and Captain Allen met one last time in person to develop their battle plans when they arrived at Sikorsky's Planet. After three hours of debate, they unanimously decided to initiate a blockade of Sikorsky's Planet and stop all incoming and outgoing space craft until Vladimir Sikorsky agreed to step down. If a space battle was going to occur, Admiral Khan did not want to be the aggressor.

When they first stopped at the moon called Robert Andrews, Khan issued the order for all children and non-combatants to be left on the lunar settlement for their own protection. He sent his wives and children there. His parting from his wives was emotional. Khan felt love for them all, but Charsa would always be his closest. He kissed her goodbye as she boarded a Raumschiff with the other wives and their children. He waived at her as she turned to look at him one last time. She blew him a kiss before turning around and boarding the Raumschiff.

Roberta Largo bid her lover, geologist Abrahim Haddad, farewell as he boarded one of the transport ships. Similar separations were occurring throughout the Second Fleet as the exodus of children and non-combatants moved with swiftness and precision.

Targa Jara White flew one of the packed Raumschiffs from the *Rorke's Drift* to the lunar surface. On board the ship were seventy men, women and children that were not members of the military branches. Most of them were spouses that were allowed to travel with their husband or wife as the latter served on the Battle Cruiser. White's husband, Sylvester White, was one of those that was going to be left behind on Robert Andrews. He had encouraged his wife to stay with her crew and fight for the freedoms that they all desperately craved. Sylvester White was sad that his wife would be separated from him, but he had their two children to watch over in her absence.

Dia Cho and Felicia Essex said their goodbyes to their four children. They cried, hugged and cried some more. The two mothers promised the children that they would do their best to return to them as soon as possible. DLE211, DLE212 and DLE213 had met the four children and said their farewells. The children were named Dominic Cho, Marco Essex, Aura Lynda Cho and Mary Essex. Essex and Cho had given the first names to their children as tribute to their closest friends in Clovis City. All four had been created using the eggs of Cho and Essex and the sperm of Dominic Andolini. The children did not know who their father was as Cho and Essex were raising the four children as a couple. Dominic had been their friend and agreed to help them with the in vitro procedure. Cho and Essex had been fastidious in their selection of the sperm donor. Dominic was their choice and they were elated that he happily agreed to give them what they had needed.

But now, with the two women quickly moving into harm's way, they felt that there could be a possibility that the children would need their father. Cho and Essex flew to the surface of the Robert Andrews moon and met the citizens that were setting up a new life and direction for themselves.   They had successfully wiped out the Royal Family members on the planet. They were elated with their success in winning their freedom from the Glorious Leader.

Cho and Essex instructed their children that if they were not able to come get them, that they were to trust a man named Dominic Andolini. The two women did not elaborate as to why they were to accept the man. The children seemed to be emotionally fine with the arrangement. They liked Mister Jordan and his two children so staying with him was not an issue. But Essex was certain the children would become restless when the days without their mothers passed. She was reticent as she kept her opinions from Cho. They hugged the children good bye before returning to their ship to assist in the blockade of Sikorsky's Planet. Other families said their farewells as the civilian parents stayed behind to care for the offspring.

Pilot Azalia Dell flew one of the Raumschiff transports, packed with sixty men, women and children to the moon. She had watched them all bid farewell to their loved ones on the *Amistad*. Dell found herself second guessing her decision to become a traitor to the Royal Family. They had never wronged her, at least not directly. Dell had observed six other pilots indicate that they would not be a part of the blockade of Sikorsky's Planet, so they were also leaving to the sanctuary on the moon below. After landing on Robert Andrews and waiting until the last of her passengers were safely on the surface, Dell almost left to join them. At the last second she thought of her friends back on the Battle Cruiser and made the decision to return to them.

After the crews of the *Amistad, Rorke's Drift, Montenegro, Nigeria* and *New Delhi* sent the children and scientists to the moon called Robert Andrews, they continued on their mission. Within a week of leaving the others behind, the five Battle Cruisers entered the orbit of Sikorsky's Planet without incident. Admiral Khan and Captain Allen were surprised that the security towers on Sikorsky's Planet had not challenged them as to their authority to be in the region. By leaving their mission patrolling the outer solar systems, they had already disobeyed direct orders from the Glorious Leader. That alone would warrant a court martial. But they received no demands or inquiries.

Khan believed that to be odd.

The *Amistad* had a total crew of seven hundred seventy-one pilots and three hundred sixty additional crew consisting of tactical officers, weapons technicians, engineers, mechanics and enlisted men and women. The other four ships had about the same amount of crew members.

The fact that they had not met with resistance left the five commanders confused. Each of the five ships had over seven hundred fifty Allen Corporation Fighter Type CC76A3 space craft which they launched and created a ring around the planet. Admiral Khan also ordered that all of the Raumschiffs on the five Battle Cruisers be launched to guard the rear and the flanks of the fleet. All of the crews were vigilant for attack.

Khan sat in the Captain's seat of the *Montenegro* and contacted the other four Captains. He had their four images displayed before him in his three dimensional viewer. Captain Allen had dressed in his formal uniform and indicated he was ready for action. Newly field promoted Captain Dana Del Rey reported that she was ready for action. Likewise, new Captains Gloria Ciara Harvard of the *Nigeria* and Talisia Nora Rogers of the *New Delhi* announced combat ready. They all listened as Admiral Khan sent an ultimatum to the Glorious Leader to surrender.

Privately, Allen and Khan had met with Rogers to discuss whether or not she should continue with her part as a member of the insurrection. Rogers had come from a prominent family on Mars that owned numerous office buildings and high rise apartment dwellings. She had been born and raised there and attended the Martian Academy to obtain her commission. She was more than capable to perform as the Captain of a Battle Cruiser due to her skills as a pilot and tactical experience. Rogers had no grudge or personal grievances against the Glorious Leader. After Khan and Allen had offered to let Rogers leave the fleet and go home to her family, Rogers declined. She told both men that she had reviewed the evidence presented to them and that led her to agree with their goal to remove the Sikorsky's from power.

Next, Allen and Khan met with Gloria Harvard and gave her the option of leaving the confrontation. Allen believed that Harvard would most certainly be reticent to be involved in the war to remove the Sikorsky's. The main reason was that her father, Golden Harvard, had been promoted to a high cabinet position under the Sikorsky United Nations scheme. Going to war against the Sikorsky family would be akin to turning on her own family. Gloria Harvard made the decision to stay on for many reasons. Her top reason was that she was in fear for her family due to the emotional instability of the Glorious Leader. She felt she needed to help in the effort to establish a new government and leadership so that her father and her large sibling group would never suffer the bi-polar outbursts of Vladimir Sikorsky.

After the ultimatum had been given, they waited all of fifteen minutes for the answer of the Glorious Leader. He issued a death sentence against all of them.

"The people cannot tolerate instability and insurrection," Vladimir Sikorsky said in a prepared statement that was broadcast to the eight solar systems of the United Nations of Earth. "My leadership is needed now more than ever. The fact that many of the high ranking officers in the Space Command believe that they can follow the lead of a Zhydovka to seize power should be frightening to us all. I have ordered that the First Fleet under the command of my son, Admiral Perdiccas, to meet the treasonous members of the Second Fleet and kill them all.   As we demonstrated by our decisiveness with the revolution on Chronos, we now will remind humanity that we will never show weakness. Challenge our government and you will be hunted down and executed as criminals."

The entire world heard the edict from the Glorious Leader.

Marco Andolini had been field promoted by Captain Allen before entering the binary solar system for Sikorsky's Planet.   He had given him the rank of Lieutenant and placed him in charge of Amistad Squadron A. Marco had command of forty-one other pilots. He went over the battle plans with his squadron as they prepared for the blockade of the planet. He had thought about making an attempt to contact his parents, his brother and other siblings. But contact with anyone outside of the Fleet was declared too dangerous by Admiral Khan. Marco resisted the urge to use his holo-com device to let his family know what he was involved in.

Ellen Benson had also been promoted by Allen and placed in command of *Amistad* Squadron B. She had also fought the urge to contact her family. She resolved herself that her actions as a traitor were for the good of her family. If they could successfully disrupt the economic stability of the planet below and force the Glorious Leader to peacefully step down, then the sacrifice would be worth it. She had not told Marco that she was pregnant and felt that news could wait. She did not want to add any more emotional to the man she had grown to love. When the revolution was over she would break the news to him. For now, Benson kept quiet and motivated the forty-one pilots under her command.

Captain Allen ordered that the first five squadrons of Allen Corporation Fighter Type CC76A3 space craft begin to patrol their assigned areas of space. Marco led his pilots to the Docking Area of the *Amistad*, had them suit up in their enviro-suits and ordered them all to ready their space craft. He took a roll call and endured the off the cuff remarks of Patricia Dwyer about wanting to take her vibrator along with her on the mission. Marco took special care in making sure that Ezra Tulley and Mary Winston had their security checks done correctly. Both of the pilots seemed terrified about their first combat situation and Admiral Seward had taught Marco that scared pilots made mistakes. Plus, he could not forget that Tina Martinson had panicked in a combat situation and that had cost her life.

Marco found Benson in the Docking Bay moments before his squadron was to launch. She was putting on her enviro-suit and standing next to her Allen Corporation

Fighter Type CC76A3 space craft. Marco pushed his way through the crowds of mechanics and engineers that were running this way and that. He had to step over several tool kit boxes and large supply boxes to get to Benson. She smiled when she saw him approach her. He took her in his arms and kissed her.

"I did not want to leave without telling you how much I love you," Marco said loud enough for her to hear over all of the activity.

Benson kissed him back. "I love you Marco, more than anything. You be careful out there. The First Fleet is supposed to be the best in the Space Command."

"I know. You watch your back." He pulled her close to him and whispered into her ear. "If we are getting our butts kicked out there, rendezvous with me on the other side of the farthest star. I will be there waiting for you."

"You mean run away from the fight?" Benson was a bit stunned that he would suggest such a thing.

"No, I mean that if things are going so badly for us that all is lost then we need to regroup." Marco held her hands in his. "If the First Fleet is able to destroy our host Battle Cruisers and we have no place else to go, then meet me there. Lead as many pilots as you can to that location. Promise me you will be there."

"I promise you I will be there," Benson told him. She had never seen Marco act so concerned. His normal demeanor was clouded by his feelings of gloom in what they were about to attempt. A blockade of a planet with several space stations and an elite fleet of Battle Cruisers guarding her was a challenge. They each held one another as the computerized voice announced that the squadrons would soon be launching.

The two lovers released each other and Benson watched as Marco ran back toward his ship. She smiled briefly and then kneeled down to pick up her enviro-suit helmet. She touched her stomach and took in a deep breath before climbing on board her small space craft. Benson hoped that they were not all about to be wiped out by the pilots of the First Fleet. She prayed that many of those pilots would agree with the position of Admiral Khan and Captain Allen and join their quest to end the rule of the Glorious Leader. Benson sat in her cockpit and began performing her engine and systems check. In moments she would be flying in space and waiting for the inevitable attack.

Within thirty minutes, Marco was piloting his small space craft from the belly of the Battle Cruiser *Amistad* and out into space. He dispersed his squadron out and ordered all of his pilots to keep a look out for any hostile action. He felt in his stomach that the words of the Glorious Leader had to be taken seriously. He had ruled for over two hundred years. He would not give up his power without a fight.

Del Rey had her crew motivated. She gave them a fiery speech about freedom and justice which seemed to inspire them. She ordered her chief pilot, Targa Jara White to lead the first five fighter squadrons out into space. Del Rey had her Battle Cruiser patrolling the northern quadrant of Sikorsky's Planet. Her mission was to not allow any space craft in our out. Admiral Khan had demanded a strict quarantine and Del Rey was determined to follow her orders. She heard the threats made by the Glorious Leader against them. She grimaced and realized that confrontation was a certainty. She instructed her crew to be vigilant and seek out any sign that the First Fleet was coming toward them.

CHAPTER SIX

The Command Station of the United Nations Space Command Battle Cruiser *Remagen* was bustling with activity. Several weapons and computer technicians were climbing up and down the ladders to the second and third levels to make preparations for the arrival of their Admiral. They had been placed on the highest defense condition which meant they were going to war. It was not a training exercise. The adrenaline level of each crew member was spiking at their highest levels.

In the sixth level of the *Remagen* was the large Docking Bays which had one thousand Allen Corporation Fighter Type CC76A5 space craft waiting for battle. The A5's were faster than the A3's and were only manufactured for use in the Glorious Leader's First Fleet and some of his private ships. The mechanics and engineers were rapidly working on each ship to mount armor piercing rockets and extra laser batteries. Many of the pilots were donning their gold colored enviro-suits

One of those pilots was Lieutenant Jayne Starr. Starr had studied to be a pilot and officer at the well-respected Academy on Sikorsky's Planet. To gain admission to that prestigious Academy, Starr and to have perfect grades in her school work and score well on all of her aptitude tests. She also had to obtain letters of recommendation from many high ranking officials in the General Assembly of her home planet, New Edinburgh. Starr was tall with sandy blonde hair and light brown eyes. She was slender and spent a minimum of three days a week in the gymnasium to keep her weight down as was required by Space Command regulations. She came from a large sibling group and was the first to leave her family to live on another planet. Her siblings did not obtain high grade marks as she had and ended up attending other universities and Academies. A year earlier, she had lost a younger brother named Roy to an attack by some assassins named Ragnarsson. Starr had initially felt guilty that she had not been on her home world to protect her fallen brother. She missed him and hoped that she would never have to lose another sibling. Now that she was in the middle of a war, Starr had that worry for her sister that was now serving on the *Remagen* with her. She was determined to find her sister before they were sent off to battle.

Starr was in command of her own Flight Squadron of over forty ships and pilots. She had been given the orders from her Captain and had relayed those orders to her pilots. They were to pursue and kill the enemy. Starr was a bit perplexed as she had learned that the enemy was the entire compliment of the Second Fleet under Admiral Khan. They were to fight and kill their own military personnel. Starr had attempted to confirm her orders with the Captain of the *Remagen*. She finally got him to respond to her on her personal communication device. She smiled as the red image of Captain Trent Janssen appeared before her.

"Lieutenant, I am extremely busy here," Captain Janssen told her.

"Yes sir. I am sorry for the interruption." Starr said over the loud noises being made by the engineers and mechanics. "I received order that we are to annihilate the Second Fleet and take no prisoners. Is this correct, sir?"

Janssen nodded, "Yes, Lieutenant. Admiral Khan and his crew have declared war against the Glorious Leader. They have surrounded Sikorsky's Planet and announced a blockade of all ships coming or going. We must do several things. We must break the Blockade and break the spirit of all those that desire revolution. The eight solar systems cannot take regime change at this time. We must crush Admiral Khan and all of his crew members as an example to the rest of humanity."

Starr was about to respond when Captain Janssen's image faded away. She closed her device and began to look around the activity in the Docking Bay. She finally saw her sister, Renee Starr, who was barking orders at her own squadron to get ready. The two Starr sisters had attended different Academies. While Jayne had learned to pilot at the Sikorsky Academy, Renee had studied at Clovis Academy. Renee had made high marks on her pilot examinations and was drafted by Captain Janssen to serve on his ship. It was considered an honor to serve on the First Fleet as only the best were selected.

While Jayne Starr had not been involved with any men for the last two years, Renee had the attention of one of the male pilots, a Lieutenant Commander named Bill Rice and an engineering technician named Franklin Kustler. Jayne wondered how her sister could play off two men at the same time and keep them coming back for more when there were so many more available women to men. Jayne would jokingly tell Renee that she must have game to keep the two men wrapped around her little finger.

Jayne pushed through the crowd of mechanics and other pilots as she made her way to her sister's location. When she was about ten feet away she called out for her. "Renee!"

Renee heard her name and turned to see her sister. The two women hugged. Renee was similar looking to her sister and had a sex appeal to her that attracted others. Renee was always more conscious of spending more time with makeup and grooming her hair. She also had a good eye for fashion and would dress provocatively on her off duty time. Jayne was the opposite as she was content to wear baggy sweats and put her hair under a baseball cap. But in uniform, both sisters followed regulation and had their flight suits pressed, their boots shined and their hair pinned up.

"Jayne! Is this for real? Are we really going to fight our own people?" Renee asked her sister. She was shaking with either fear or excitement. She had never seen real action before. All of her tests had been conducted with a simulator or over the Forbidden Region on planet New Edinburgh. Jayne on the other hand had led a squadron attack against a small band of pirate ships at the edge of the solar system. It had been a highly publicized battle and Jayne defeated the pirates, killing most of them and forcing the remainder to surrender and face trial. Jayne received the Space Command Medal of Valor for that action. In a later event, Jayne had been sent to one of the terra formed planets in the solar system to transport one of the sons of the Glorious Leader to make a speech at the General Assembly there. There was an assassination attempt and Jayne was able to shoot the would be killer in the chest with her laser pistol, saving the life of the son of the Glorious Leader. Jayne received the United Nations Medal of Honor for that act.

As they were hugging, Jayne whispered into her sister's ear. "Renee, if things get too crazy out there, bug out and I mean it."

"You mean run?" Renee could not believe that her highly decorated sister would suggest such a thing.

"Dad is still heartbroken over losing Roy. How do you think he will be if we die, too?" Jayne reminded her of their younger brother that had been killed by the attack on Clovis Academy the last year. "You go to the dark side of the planet and hide. Better yet, get to the other side of the binary suns. If anyone ever asks you it was due to engine trouble. Understand?"

Renee looked her sister in the eyes, "You are an Ace Pilot. You have nine kills to your name. I want to be like you, Jayne. I want to be an Ace, so that means I have to blast five of those revolutionaries out of the sky."

"We will be in outer space, Renee." Jayne corrected her. "Have you ever seen a human get swept out into space without an enviro-suit? Because I have. It is horrible. These are our people out there. This isn't some aggressive alien race we are about to fight. This is humans against humans. We may have friends and former classmates on those ships. Can you live with yourself if you killed someone you cared about? Can you?"

Before Renee could respond to her sister they heard the announcement of Marine Corps Colonel Aldo Ortega. His voice was echoing throughout the entire ship announcing that the Planetary Defense Command had just launched three thousand Allen Corporation Fighter Type CC76A4 space craft to intercept the fighters of the Second Fleet. The war was beginning in earnest.

"You see, Jayne? We may not even see any action. Those Planetary Defense pilots might kill all of the rebel pilots off before we get sent in. You are worried over nothing. I can fly just fine, sis. Do not worry about me."

Jayne grabbed her arm and held her close to her. "Do not underestimate the enemy, Renee. They are fighting for something. They want freedom. People have been willing to die for that ideal for thousands of years. An adversary that is not afraid to give her life for freedom is very dangerous. You watch your back out there."

Jayne stormed off and jogged toward her squadron area. Her sister was full of delusions of grandeur. Jayne hoped that Renee did not get herself killed.

Captain Trent Janssen sat down in his Captain's seat on the Command Station of the *Remagen*. He was met by Marine Corps Colonel Aldo Ortega and his Executive Officer, Lieutenant Commander Shauna Gannon. All three of them were members of the Royal Family. They were honored to be the leaders of the flagship of the First Fleet. The *Remagen* was one of the best Battle Cruisers in the Space Command. She had six levels as opposed to the majority of other Battle Cruiser's which had only five. The *Remagen* had smaller fighter ships and Raumschiff's than the average Battle Cruiser and they had more weaponry. They also had the best officers from the Academies. To serve in the First Fleet, one had to achieve the best test scores.

Janssen did not like the idea of killing everyone in the Second Fleet. Admiral Khan was a personal friend and had attended one of his weddings. Killing him was not going to be easy for Janssen. But standing by and doing nothing to prevent the end of the Sikorsky Regime was something Janssen could not do. Based on the two options before him, Janssen determined that his old friend would have to die.

"Status report?" Janssen demanded to his crew.

"Weapons and security are ready for battle, sir." Ortega bellowed out.

"All pilots are prepared to engage the enemy." Gannon reported.

"Estimated time for the Planetary Defense ships intercept the Second Fleet?" Janssen turned to Ortega.

"Thirty minutes," Ortega responded.

"Commander Gannon! Order all of our fighter ships to prepare for launch in fifteen minutes, just in case any of those other fighters break through." Janssen told her. "The Planetary Defense space fighters should weaken up the fighters of the Second Fleet enough to make their Battle Cruisers open for direct attack. This is war!"

At that moment, all of the crew on the Command Station jumped to attention. One of the four Marine Corps guards at the elevator lifts yelled out: "Admiral on the Bridge!"

Admiral Philip Perdicas calmly walked onto the Command Station and looked over his staff. It had been eight months since their last action. The crew seemed to be motivated and focused on their mission. Perdicas smiled at his fellow Royal Family members.

"Carry on," Perdicas instructed the crew members. He looked up at the third level of the Command Station and spied upon a young Ensign that was working the computers.   She was an attractive looking woman with dark hair and skin. "Patch me in to Admiral Khan."

"Yes Admiral," the young Ensign responded. After a few moments everyone saw the holographic three dimensional view of the Admiral of the Second Fleet before them.

"Admiral Perdicas," Khan said softly. When Khan had finished his education at the Academy his first assignment had been as a fighter pilot under Admiral Perdicas in the First Fleet. Khan served under Perdicas for ten years and even became one of his personal aerial protectors. Khan excelled under Perdicas and was promoted three times by him. In his heart, Khan did not want to have to fight his former mentor. He admired Perdicas greatly and felt a sense of loyalty to the man.

"Admiral Khan, you are looking well, my friend," Perdicas told him.

"As are you, Philip." Khan responded. "I gather

that this is not a social call."

"No, I am afraid it is not."   Perdicas sighed and began to pace around Khan's image. "My father, the Glorious Leader, has decreed that you and all of your crew from the Second Fleet are to be executed for your acts of treason."

"I understand, my friend."

"Due to our long standing friendship, I believe I can appeal to my father for leniency on behalf of your crew." Perdicas said. "But only if you surrender now. As for you and Captain Allen I doubt that I would be successful in intervening on your behalf."

Khan was silent as he absorbed the information. Khan had always believed that had Perdicas been able to rise up to the position of Glorious Leader that there would have been new laws that would have endorsed and embraced freedom for the people. Perdicas was doing his job and Khan had no qualms with that. Conflict by combat was inevitable.

"I appreciate your kind offer my friend," Khan told Perdicas softly. "My people are not willing to surrender. I ask as a counter-offer that the Glorious Leader step down and appoint you as temporary Secretary General of the UN so that we may all negotiate a peaceful resolution to this.

Everyone knows you Philip and they all respect you. If you were to become the leader, I could begin discussions to end the blockade."

Perdicas had never allowed himself the luxury of considering ousting his father from power. Perdicas had done many of the things that Vladimir Sikorsky had been accused of, including using body parts of young girls to replace his own aging internal organs. It would take just a few hours for the new regime to uncover the crimes that Perdicas committed over the previous century. He could not allow that to happen.

"I must humbly reject your gracious counter-offer," Perdicas said. "I suggest that you and your crew members prepare yourselves. Contact any loved ones you may have and tell them good bye."

"Thank you, Admiral." Khan responded and bowed to him. "You shall always have my utmost respect."

Perdicas waited as the image of Khan disappeared. He looked at Janssen. "Patch me into the rest of the First Fleet."

"You are on, sir," Janssen said.

"This is Admiral Perdicas. We anticipate our Planetary Defense System fighter ships will engage the enemy in fifteen minutes. If any of the opposing space craft are able to break through the fighters and advance on our Battle Cruisers then we will have to take offensive action. At that point we will launch all of our fighters to finish them off." Perdicas paused for dramatic effect. "My father, the Glorious Leader, has decreed that there can be no survivors. All of the Second Fleet must be wiped out. The eight solar systems must witness the slaughter so that other like-minded treasonous citizens will be discouraged. Make certain all of your crew members understand that if they spare anyone, they will die in their place. The entire population of humanity must be taught that insurrection will only end in death."

Perdicas motioned to Janssen to end the communication.

"So it is war, then?" Shauna Gannon asked.

Perdicas nodded to her, "Yes, my dear cousin. But I would say it will be more like a slaughter. Khan and his followers are as good as dead. Let us observe how they handle themselves against our pawns."

On the Command Station of the Battle Cruiser *Montenegro*, Admiral Khan sat in silence. His command crew watched him in silence as well. He finally rose to his feet and faced them all. Their faces were full of hope as they waited for his words of wisdom and encouragement.

"I cannot lie to any of you," Khan began. "We may all die here in the next few hours. If we are to survive this battle, we must dig down deep into our hearts and souls. We have to fight like madmen. We have to fight like demons. It is our only way to live. You all understand?"

"Yes, Admiral!" The rousing response came.

"Then get to your battle stations. Launch all fighters and Raumschiffs." Khan ordered. "This is it!"

CHAPTER SEVEN

From the opposite side of the binary suns, Doctor Nicolette Rosenburg was lying in bed with her lover, Charles Bennington. They had made love after listening to the broadcasted back and forth threats between the soon to be adversaries. Bennington had left two of the Love-Easter clones in the pilot section of their Raumschiff as he and his attractive lover spent some quality time together.

"This really is about to happen," Nicolette said quietly as she cuddled in his arms.

"It was what your sister promised," Bennington stroked her hair. "I hope she can get reinforcements in soon. Allen and Khan are excellent commanders but so are Perdicas and the Sikorsky's. They won't fight fair."

Nicolette was about to respond when they heard each of their holo-com's beeping. She rolled over in the small bed and reached her right hand out to the dresser where her device was beckoning for her attention. She flipped it open.

"Yes"

"We found something," one of the Love-Easters told her.

"What is it?"

"A communication beacon. We estimate it to be two hundred ten years old."

"Bring it in."

"We are," the Replicant said. "We sent Barry and Ralph Garrison out in enviro-suits to do a spacewalk and retrieve it. They just let us know that they have secured it. We should have it inside the ship in about thirty minutes. I will let you know."

Nicolette closed her holo-com shut and rolled back and faced Bennington. "Do you think it is from the Calypso?"

"We should be so lucky. If it is, then we need to get ready to broadcast the contents to the rest of the eight solar systems." Bennington kissed her. "I wonder how the rest of humanity would take to hearing the last words of Robert Andrews now."

CHAPTER EIGHT

There were over twenty-one million people living in the nation state called the Nevada Territory. It had formed when the old United States of America collapsed from the runaway debt that had accumulated and could never be repaid. Nevada formed a new nation by joining the northern California territory and Oregon to make a new nation. The citizens of the newly formed nation drafted a Constitution and began electing a President and legislature. The newly formed state signed a memorandum of agreement with the United Nations and submitted to the ultimate rule of the Glorious Leader, as did all of the other nations on Earth.

Cora Lima Sandoval was the nineteenth elected President of the Nevada Territory. She was a trial lawyer in her early career and had served as an elected Judge for four years. She then ran for Nevada National Senate and won her district's seat. After serving in the Nevada Senate for eight years, Cora Sandoval sought her political party's nomination for President of the nation state. She won in the primary elections easily and then won the Presidency by a landslide against two other opponents. Her conservative fiscal policies balanced the budget of the Nevada Territory and she was able to amass a surplus for a Rainy Day Fund. Although she was tight fisted when it came to government expenditures she was the first to tell others that the truly needy must always be helped.   Cora Sandoval was hailed as an example of a great President by other nation states. She was re-elected as President in the following election cycle.

Sandoval was now in her early sixties.   Her husband, Raul Sandoval, was also a trial lawyer and about the same age as his wife. They had met when they were building their law practices in Reno, Nevada.   Their marriage had been full of ups and downs over the decades, but they stuck together through the good and the bad. They had five children, all girls, which were either beginning their careers or in college preparing to become productive members of the human race.   The Sandoval family was looked upon with great respect in their nation. Cora Sandoval governed with fairness to her fellow citizens. To her, public service was an honor and she approached her duties with humility.

The Nevada Territory was celebrating its' bi-centennial and the mood of the citizens was one of unity and joy. There were festivities occurring in the streets and neighborhoods throughout the Territory. The celebration was not so much for the bi-centennial, but for the recent declaration of cessation from the United Nations and separation from the dictatorship of Vladimir Sikorsky.

President Sandoval and her husband had been heavily involved in the Empire United Nations. President Sandoval had sent her sister, Elena Lima Nobis to serve as Nevada Territory Ambassador to the UN. Nobis had made many influential contacts and friends during her four years of service in that position. She also was exposed to some terrible and horrifying truths. Nobis, while serving on the UN Crimes Against Children Sub-Committee, learned that thousands of teen-age girls had been disappearing without a trace. Ambassador Nobis took it upon herself to authorize funds to begin investigations into some of the tragic and unexplained missing teenage women. Nobis selected five specific cases, believing if those could be solved then there may be a way to solve the others. Nobis felt the crimes were all somehow connected.

Sadly, Nobis was correct in her assumptions.

Her investigators were able, after a year of digging,

to come up with eye witnesses, security camera video feeds and actual photographs from private citizens that showed the women being stalked or followed at their last known locations. The photographs revealed the image of two men. And these two men were the same person in all five of the cases Nobis had selected to have investigated. She took the photographs to the computerized identification centers and could not get any resolution as to the identities of the men.

Nobis then had her staff seek out the identity of the men by questioning individuals that were involved in the illegal drug trade. They further interviewed, off the record, suspected slave trade witnesses that were willing to talk, as long as they were anonymous. After the extensive inquiry was completed, Nobis had two names.

Dell Ragnarsson and David Rosenburg.

Nobis and her team of investigators delved into the backgrounds of these two men and found that David Rosenburg had died in the Blood Moon Incident while fighting with Yuri Gorski, Drew Harrison and Les Gillis. David Rosenburg had replaced his human bone structure with metals so that caused the three cadets great difficulty in vanquishing him. Before the Blood Moon, David Rosenburg had a reputation for being a loyal son to his father, Alfred. David Rosenburg had also been a major player in the illegal slave trade market for alien beings and humans. He was further suspected to be involved in the production and distribution of Red Dust which was an illegal drug.

Dell Ragnarsson had also been identified as one of the participants on the Blood Moon. His Raumschiff had been destroyed in the battle but his body had never been recovered. Many speculated as to whether or not he had died or somehow escaped. Nobis and her staff uncovered Ragnarsson's history, at least what little was available. Ragnarsson had covered his tracks well. Most of the information regarding Ragnarsson came from his daughter, Ella, who was now a convicted prisoner enroute to the Prison Planet Cootron. According to Ella, Dell was a loyal assassin for the Rosenburg's and Sikorsky's. Dell had killed thousands for the Glorious Leader and the Rosenburg family. Most of Ragnarsson's many children had followed his example and became hired killers themselves. Some of them had been apprehended and others had died while attempting to kill the students at Clovis Academy.

But Dell Ragnarsson and David Rosenburg had performed yet another function for the Glorious Leader and the Rosenburg's. They sought out young women to be used to give birth to many offspring for the family leaders.

Ragnarsson and Rosenburg would kidnap the women and take them to Sikorsky's Planet for the Glorious Leader, or to New Edinburgh for the Rosenburg family or to planet Cootron for the Sikorsky's that ruled that earth-like planet. Once the women had given a few sets of children, generally a dozen or so in total, the women were taken to the dungeons where a shop of terror awaited them. The women were kept conscious as their bodies were skinned and their internal organs were forcibly removed. No medicine was given for pain as the Glorious Leader loved to hear their screams as they were sliced open.

And then their body parts were used to replace the aging body parts of members of the Royal Family. The kidnaped women were used to give the Royal Family members immortality.

Their children were raised to be loyal Royal Family members and to become leaders themselves in either the political or military realm. The Glorious Leader had found that having his descendants in high positions was the best way to preserve his two hundred year rule.

Nobis and her staff uncovered one of the dungeons in vast underground chamber located in the eastern North American continent. They found the hollowed out carcasses of women that had been used for birthing vessels and then their body parts harvested for some Royal Family member in need. Nobis and her staff were sickened by their discovery.

Nobis took her findings, which when printed on paper took up over four thousand pages. She was angry when the Secretary General of the UN on Earth, Natasha Sikorsky, rebuked her for wasting the money of the taxpayers to look into such a trivial issue. Natasha Sikorsky was a Royal and Nobis was not surprised that the woman refused to acknowledge the research and the evidence.

Nobis, realizing that the Royal Family might target her and her team, returned to Nevada Territory on her private transport. While in flight, she sent by computerized document sharing functions all of her findings to her sister, Cora. Nobis also sent her findings to some of the Ambassadors at the UN that she believed would be angered by the evidence. Nobis and her ship never made it back to her home city of Reno, Nevada. Her craft was blown up in what the news media labeled as a separatist attack. All eleven on board the craft died instantly.

The President of Nevada Territory, Cora Sandoval, received the internet coded message and the attached reports sent to her by Nobis. After reading the reports,

Sandoval made a fateful decision. She released all of the findings of her sister to the media and to the people of her nation state. She used the murder of her sister and the evidence of the internal organ harvesting by the Royal Family to advocate cessation from Sikorsky rule.

The majority of the people were so incensed by the images of the dead women that they readily followed the popular President Sandoval and announced cessation.

As the celebrations in the streets continued to the early morning, President Sandoval and her husband sat in the privacy of their eighty floor Presidential mansion in Las Vegas, Nevada. Their police force had rounded up all of the Royal Family members in Nevada Territory and had them detained for trial. They shared a bottle of imported Moscato and listened to the people sing songs and cheer their independence on the streets below.

They did not realize that night was to be their last.

Pravda Sikorsky and Ulla Ragnarsson had been able to gain access to the Presidential mansion by using old architectural drawings from when the building had been constructed. The two women snuck in, under cover of the dark night, while the people cheered and made noise loud enough to easily cover their entrance to an old emergency exit at the basement of the mansion. Ulla had to use special tools to cut her way into the emergency exit. The sounds of the drilling were drowned out by the screams of joy on the streets and the fireworks exploding in the night sky.

Once they were inside, Pravda methodically cut the throats of the few security guards on the basement level. The guards were members of the elite police group Nevada Bureau of Investigations, or the NBI. Pravda found them to be easy to kill and questioned in her mind the competency of the remained of the Nevada law enforcement services if the NBI were the best. She led Ulla to the elevator lifts and to the eightieth floor to complete their mission. Vladimir Sikorsky, had issued an edict of death to all that rebelled against his rule.

Pravda and Ulla met little resistance on the way to the top of the Presidential mansion. They had to dispatch four more NBI officers before entering the spacious living quarters of President Cora Sandoval and her husband.

The two female assassins crept in silence as they explored the kitchen area, the den, the study and the bed room of the Sandoval's. By the process of elimination, Ulla deduced that the President and her husband were on the balcony. They slowly moved in the direction of the balcony and found the Sandoval's sitting in leather sofas, drinking their Moscato and listening to the screams of joy below.

Pravda moved in first, taking several fast steps toward the unsuspecting Raul Sandoval. Before he realized what was happening, Pravda had kicked him with her left foot, out of his comfortable sofa and rolling to the carpeted balcony. His wine glass sailed into the air, over the five foot tall brick wall and falling downward for eighty floors before crashing on top of the head of a random citizen.

Raul Sandoval was not the kind of man that cursed. But, the surprise attack caused him to blurt out an expletive. Cora Sandoval was attacked from behind by Ulla. Wrapping her garrote around Cora Sandoval's throat, Ulla lifted the President to her feet. Cora struggled for breath as Ulla tightened the piano wire around her unprotected throat.

Pravda jumped onto Raul Sandoval, driving her left knee into his solar plexus and knocking the air from him. He could not scream.

"I suppose the two of you knew you would not get away with your acts of treason." Pravda said as she drew out her foot long knife. "After we kill you both, we are going to hunt down your daughters and grandchildren and kill them too. There will be nothing left of you family by this time tomorrow."

Cora could not cry for help and watched as the woman cut open Raul's pants and then sliced off his testicles and penis. Raul was able to let loose a cry of pain just before Pravda gutted him by slicing open his stomach, just below the navel. Pravda reached into the man's wounds and pulled out his intestinal track.

Ulla pulled her garrote tighter and tighter. The piano wire sliced through the throat of the President of the Nevada Territory. Blood began to spurt out from her severed jugular vein. Ulla held the woman upright until her kicking and struggling ceased. She laid the body next to her dying husband. She nodded to Pravda. Their work was finished. They departed in silence and avoided contact with others as they escaped the mansion without detection.

Their next stop was to travel to Ireland and kill the rebellious leaders there. After that task was completed, they were to return home to Sikorsky's Planet for further instructions. They returned to their Raumschiff to find that Barry Flynn was there waiting for them.

The two women had known Flynn for several years but they were never close to the man. He had been a close confidant to the Rosenburg family and had been known to manage their slave and illegal weapons trade. He had once had a promising career in the Space Command until he was arrested for raping the daughter of his Captain. Flynn was tried and convicted at a court martial and lost his rank of Lieutenant Commander. He was going to spend fifty years in jail when he was given an offer from the Rosenburg family. They arranged for Flynn's escape in return for him working for them and earning three times his past salary. The disgraced pilot took the deal and had been a loyal employee of the Rosenburg family ever since. Flynn was a rogue and looked the part. He had not shaved in days, his dark hair had streaks of grey and hung down below his shoulders. He was a bit overweight and wore a one-piece black flight suit with a black leather jacket over it. He had a laser pistol, large knife and some stun darts attached to the web belt that was around his waist. The women had not been expecting Flynn. In fact they had not been informed that he was on Old Earth at all.

"Captain Flynn," Ulla greeted him. "This is certainly a surprise."

"Yes, for me as well." Flynn smiled as he looked the two women over. His reputation for keeping the company of under-age girls and prostitutes was well known. He had a wandering eye and seemed to appreciate the women before him far too much for their liking.

"Why are you here?" Pravda demanded. She was

not happy at the manner Flynn was staring at her chest.

"I was picking up a few more organ donors for the family," Flynn told them. For both assassins that was code for kidnaping young girls to have their internal organs ripped out for the Sikorsky family. "Well, I just received a holo-com order from John Rosenburg. He instructed me to find you two lovely ladies and get you to return to Sikorsky's Planet. Immediately."

"Why?" Ulla demanded.

"Because John and the Professor are going to launch a Red Javelin to wipe out all life on Earth," Flynn laughed. "The Glorious Leader decreed that any planet that harbors others that are part of the insurrection will be annihilated. But, they didn't want you two ladies here when the weapon arrives and detonates. So, I suggest you get a move on. Oh, and don't stop on Mars for any reason. There is a possibility of a Red Javelin being sent there, too."

"So they decided to bring down the hammer," Pravda said thoughtfully. "About damn time. These peasants are no better than farm animals. Wipe them all out and then we can start over with people that are completely loyal."

"That's the plan. Have a safe flight back home, ladies."

Flynn walked away from them and did not look back.

"He is creepy," Ulla said after Flynn was out of earshot.

"I agree. Let's do as he said. I don't want to be anywhere in this solar system when those Red Javelin weapons start activating." Pravda told her.

"How many billions are they going to kill?"

Pravda gave a thin smile. "As many as it takes to show the sheep that they have to obey us."

CHAPTER NINE

Siobhan Collins had dressed in her best skin tight black dress. It had thin straps over her shoulders and revealed much of her back and cleavage. She had her hair styled at a huge cost and but on her string of black pearls around her neck to match her black pearl dangle earrings. She spent almost an hour dressing and applying makeup for the event of a life time.

She was going to attend a party with the Glorious Leader and the majority of his children. Her boyfriend, Professor Andrew Brey O'Connell, was well connected with the Royal family and Collins was a bit surprised that they had been invited. It was the birthday celebration for the two hundred and forty-second birthday of the Glorious Leader, Vladimir Sikorsky. All of the important people on Sikorsky's Planet would be in attendance. So the pressure was on. She had to look spectacular for her love.

O'Connell arrived at her dormitory room at six p.m.

sharp and was dressed in a black tuxedo with shiny black shoes, white ruffle shirt and black bow tie. He had a white flower corsage for Collins and attached it to her dress after the two exchanged kisses.

"Siobhan you look amazing," O'Connell told her as he pulled her into his arms. "I will have to fight off every man at the party."

She laughed and massaged his arms softly. "No man compares to you, my love. I will not leave your side. Not even for a second."

They kissed again and they departed, arm in arm, to his personal Raumschiff that was waiting below in the space craft parking area. Each time Collins joined O'Connell on board his space craft she would recall her first night with him. They had made love on his ship more times than she could count and she hoped they would do so again in the near future. She enjoyed sitting as his co-pilot and watching him fly his space ship. Even though she was a medical student, she had picked up the basics for flying the space craft. O'Connell even allowed her to take the controls on occasion. The flight from the Sikorsky's Academy to the main Plaza Ballroom in the capital city took about twenty minutes. She massaged his left leg as she sat next to him in the pilot's section.

When they arrived, O'Connell escorted his lovely date out the back of his Raumschiff and toward the large Plaza Ballroom.

The Plaza Ballroom had been built two decades earlier and was about a mile from the Sikorsky Towers. The Ballroom had eight floors and three underground levels. Each of the floors had enough square foot space to equal three football fields. The outside was white with gold trim on the facades. The steps leading to the entrance were made of gold plated metal. The entrance had fifteen large sliding doors with two Military Intelligence security guards at each door. There were Doric columns separated fifteen feet apart at the top of the gold plated stair case. Collins was wide eyed at the large crowds she observed entering the building. She saw Generals and Admirals. There were several corporate board members from some of the wealthiest companies on Sikorsky's Planet. There were several wealthy Akarzdamedians as well that were dressed in the colorful one piece outfits of their culture.

She noticed that there were three couples of the aliens that originally came from planet Athena, they were grey with big black eyes, and oval shaped heads and stood under five feet tall. They had claimed that they had visited Old Earth many times over the centuries. By attending his birthday celebration, they seemed to hold no ill will toward the Glorious Leader for the way he massacred over ninety percent of their population when he had Athena invaded.

She saw Kotek's and some Harcourt's as well. All were dressed in nice dresses and tuxedos.

"I never walked on gold before," Siobhan whispered "Is it really gold?"

"Yes, it is.   Just wait until we are inside." O'Connell told her.

Collins could hear the buzz of many excited conversations in the lobby area as she passed through the security check. She was about to take O'Connell by the hand when, to her complete surprise, Lieutenant Azeem Nour approached them. Nour was in a Class A solid black uniform and had two women in similar uniforms on either side of him. The two women were both Corporals and considerably shorter than Nour.

"Ah, Lieutenant." O'Connell sounded pleased to see the officer. "Would you please escort us to our table?"

"With pleasure, Professor," Nour responded as he led Collins and O'Connell down the wide aisles toward the main escalator.

Siobhan recalled her unpleasant meeting with Nour at the café. She wondered how it was that O'Connell knew

Nour. She began to wonder if there was any connection with the three Yutong brothers as well. She did not ask any questions. She wanted to enjoy the moment. As she approached the platinum and silver plated escalator she looked upwards to the ceiling. There was a beautiful mural painted from end to end of the war against the Akarzdamedians. There were likenesses of the Glorious Leader and the other heroes grappling with enemy aliens. She admired the intricate and detailed paintings of the ancient Earth space craft that were depicted in battle with Akarzdamedian war ships. She wished she could spend hours looking over the massive artistic masterpiece.

When they arrived to the granite tiled second floor, she and O'Connell followed Nour into the nearest ball room entrance. Siobhan took in a deep breath as they were led across the ball room full of tables and thousands of people to the main stage. They walked up five stairs to ascend to the main stage which was skirted on the bottom with a white velvet blanket. She and O'Connell were going to be sitting at the long rectangular table up front with the Glorious Leader and his family. The table had seats for two hundred people and there was a podium made of platinum in the center of the rectangular table. She noticed that a few Admirals and Generals were already present. O'Connell was shaking their hands and introducing each one to Collins. Out of the corner of her eye she noticed that Nour was walking behind the stage with his two soldiers behind him.

O'Connell pulled out a chair for Siobhan and she sat down. She was excited and nervous at the same time. He had never told her that he had such strong connections to the Royal Family. She was offered a martini by a sharp dressed waitress which she readily accepted. She took a sip and noticed that O'Connell was also taking a drink from the same waitress.

"Some of the other men are really checking you out." O'Connell whispered to her.

"But there are so many other women here that are so beautiful," she responded.

"You are more attractive than any of them. Plus the red hair is not very common here on Sikorsky's Planet."

Siobhan nodded and began to pay attention. She found O'Connell was correct, several men were looking her over. She took another drink of her martini. She noticed on the seats on the ballroom below the main stage were the entire Harvard clan. Her former Dean, Golden Harvard, had all of his wives and minor children in attendance. As the newly appointed Secretary General of Education for the

United Nations it would have been expected for him to be present. Siobhan waived at Harvard but he did not see her due to many others in the large crowd walking around and obstructing his view.

What Siobhan did not know was that Harvard, his wives and children were concerned that they could be arrested at any time since Gloria Harvard had joined the insurrection against the Glorious Leader. Golden Harvard had already been interrogated by MI soldiers regarding his daughter and her part in the blockade and he claimed to have no knowledge of her joining such a lawless group. All of Harvard's wives and numerous children were likewise questioned. For now, the militzia seemed to be satisfied that the Harvard clan had nothing to do with Gloria's treasonous acts. Golden Harvard was torn between his love for his oldest daughter and his loyalty to the government. He secretly prayed for his daughter to return safely from her bad judgment call and allow him to intervene on her behalf with the Glorious Leader.

After the appetizers of boiled shell fish and red sauce were served, Space Command Admiral of Scientific Explorations Wallace Welker stood from his seat at the rectangular table and approached the podium. The crowd in the ballroom had not noticed him as the conversations continued. Welker cleared his throat into the microphone that was floating before the podium.

The crowd slowly grew quiet and looked up to the stage, theirs eyes locked on Welker. The Admiral smiled when the room became silent except for the clanking of plated and silverware.

"Thank you," Welker said softly. "Tonight is a special night. I was selected for the honor of introducing my father to you tonight. It is such an honor to see that my father is so well loved by all of you."

Welker held out his arms as if he wanted to embrace the crowd. "My father was the leader of humanity in the face of the greatest threat to our survival. He led with courage and with vision. He was tenacious, refused to surrender and when he led the military assault on this world, he won the day!"

The entire crowd rose to their feet and applauded. Welker smiled and held his hands up to the large crowd. The rousing applause slowly subsided and the crowd returned to their seats.

"And since that fateful day," Welker continued, "we have met with numerous challenges and adversaries. But my father led us to victory each and every time! We have expanded out influence from one planet to two solar systems.   Then three and then four! Today, humanity controls eight solar systems! And all due to my father!"

There was more applause. Welker waited patiently for the people to sit down again. "As you all know, there is a movement out there to replace my father."

The crowd began to boo that statement. Soon there were chants to kill those that would rise up against the Glorious Leader.

Welker smiled and nodded as the crowd chanted. He waited as the chants went on for several minutes before the crowd sat back in their seats.

"As I speak, there is a rogue fleet orbiting our planet and stopping all commerce from leaving or arriving! My father will crush these rebels!" Welker's voice was rising in volume as he spoke. "By tomorrow, the fleet of ships that are interfering with our daily operations will be eliminated!   And the man that will lead us to victory once again is my father! Your Glorious Leader! Wish him a Happy Birthday! Vladimir Sikorsky!"

Welker began applauding with the crowd. Siobhan stood up with O'Connell as they watched the gold curtains behind them slide open revealing Vladimir Sikorsky and several armed guards in black uniforms. Sikorsky led the guard to the rectangular table and began hugging each of his children and grandchildren that were honored with a seat on the stage. He hugged O'Connell and he introduced Siobhan to him. Sikorsky kissed her left hand and smiled at her as he continued to move down the line of esteemed guests.

After ten minutes of loud applause the Glorious Leader took his place behind the podium and clapped his hands for a while with the crowd.

"Thank you. Thank you. Thank you." Vladimir Sikorsky said as he motioned for the crowd to sit. "I love you all so much." Sikorsky placed his right hand over his heart in a manner indicating his love for the people. "Thank you. Please sit. Please. Thank you."

Siobhan sat down next to O'Connell and noticed the room was silent.

"My loyal and loving citizens. You honor me with your presence here tonight. I love each and every one of you," Sikorsky began his speech. "Sadly, many of my children and grandchildren could not attend tonight because a rebellion has begun. My son, Admiral Perdicas, is out there in space preparing to fight to preserve our way of life. Many of my other sons and daughters have been ambushed and killed. I have dispatched others to regain order and control on Cootron, Mars, Old Earth, Athena, and many other moons. I wish they were all here to celebrate with us tonight."

"We love you Glorious Leader!" A woman shouted from a table in the back.

"And I love you," Sikorsky responded. "Tonight I announce that the individuals that have brought this war to our doorstep will all die. By the morning the fleet of five Battle Cruisers that orbit this planet will be annihilated. In addition, the people of Cootron, Old Earth, Mars, Athena, New Berlin, the moon called Robert Andrews, the moon of Old Earth and several of the other terra formed worlds and moons will be wiped out. We killed all of the criminals on the moon Chronos. I now authorize wiping out all of the other locations that have announced treason. They will all die!"

The crowd began chanting and cheering. Siobhan noticed that Golden Harvard, his wives and children were looking at each other with concern over the tone of the speech. O'Connell was cheering with the crowd. She narrowed her eyes at him in disbelief. The Glorious Leader just said that he was going to have several billion people killed. That was not something to cheer. Siobhan began to feel extremely uncomfortable.

"And my loyal citizens, the instrument of the

destruction of these criminals will be completed through the usage of the weapons created your beloved Professor!" Sikorsky announced to roaring applause. "Please, Andrew, please. Tell the people how we shall restore order to the United Nations."

Siobhan's jaw opened from disbelief as the man she loved, O'Connell, stood up and walked to the podium. She watched as Sikorsky and O'Connell hugged and kissed each other on the cheeks. O'Connell walked to the podium and waved to the crowd. He was grinning and pulled out a few note cards from the breast pocket of his tuxedo.

"I bring to the Glorious Leader the greatest birthday present I could create," O'Connell told the crowd. "I created a weapon that I named Red Javelin. After the fleet of the treasonous Admiral Khan are destroyed we will launch those weapons to wipe out all human life on each of the moons and planets the Glorious Leader just listed. Billions will die. But their deaths will only make us stronger!"

The crowd was standing and applauding. Siobhan was covering her mouth in stunned silence. She felt as if she would start vomiting at any moment. The man she loved, the man she had been giving herself to each night, was a mass murderer. It took all of her willpower to keep from crying. She could feel her hands shaking as his words cut through her like a knife.

O'Connell waved to the crowd before he hugged Sikorsky once again. The Glorious Leader approached the podium once again and was waving to the massive crowd. O'Connell was walking toward Siobhan with a huge smile on his face. She fought the urge to run away. She let O'Connell hug and kiss her as he sat down. She felt as if her skin would crawl off her body when he touched her. The waiters were delivering the main course of steak, grilled tomato, and several greens that were indigenous to Sikorsky's Planet and sautéed corn and carrots. Siobhan knew she would not be able to eat. She wanted to run away to find her friend Julia Steiner and tell her what had happened.

She looked out toward the crowd as she could not bring herself to look at O'Connell or Sikorsky. She found herself struggling to breathe due to the emotional turmoil she was experiencing. As she looked over the crowd she heard some shouts and screams. She turned her attention toward the noise. She saw three Akarzdamedians charging the stage, each carrying strange looking pistols in their hands.

And they were firing them at the people on the

stage. Siobhan felt herself pulled to the ground by the strong arms of O'Connell. As she was being pulled downward she saw three women in black uniforms rushing the Glorious Leader and jumping in front of him. The three women took the blasts from the weapons to save Sikorsky. Siobhan could hear the high pitched screams of the three women as their bodies were lifted into the air and their bones were dissolved. Their flesh, muscle, blood and internal organs fell to the floor like pudding. Siobhan screamed when she saw the mounds of lifeless flesh on the floor.

The three Akarzdamedians did not get of any other shots. Azeem Nour and several soldiers opened fire on the assassins with their laser rifles. The three aliens were blown apart by the laser blasts. The crowd was screaming and panicking.

Siobhan felt herself being lifted up by a set of strong arms. She struggled with Lieutenant Dong Yutong as he was carrying her off the stage and following his two brothers who were covering O'Connell as they made their escape.

"Let me go!" Siobhan protested.

"No ma'am. The Professor says you are his," Dong responded and held her tighter. She continued to attempt to struggle until Dong injected her in the neck with a stun dart. She went limp immediately and watched helplessly as the man carried her toward O'Connell's personal space craft.

Golden Harvard had his wives and children hide underneath their tables to avoid being caught in the crossfire or be trampled on by the panic stricken guests. People were running, screaming and knocking each other to the floor. Harvard held two of his five year old daughters close to him as the screams continued. He had heard from his old friend, Admiral Seward, that the Glorious Leader sent the Battle Cruiser *Lysander* to New Edinburgh to take control of the military and the local government. Many of Harvard's friends had died, including Sigebert Evart. He saw that his wives were holding on to the youngest children and his teenage children were helping in that task.

Julia Steiner had decided to enjoy the cool breeze of the evening from the river that flowed down the center of Sikorsky's City. She had attempted to contact her other friends on the planet, Angelique LeClair, Clark Blundell and William Windfohr with no luck. The three seemed to be busier than she had been as of late. Steiner found herself missing her friends from New Edinburgh as she walked the streets in silence. She stepped aside a few times as families of humans and Akarzdamedians alike walked past her.

Steiner let her mind wander back to her days at Clovis Academy and the year she referred to as her year of innocence, her first year as a collegiate freshman. She was brought into the Gorski Gang and met Drew Harrison. She was sleeping with him within weeks of their first meeting. Steiner wondered if she had loved him at that time or she spent each night in his bed out of loneliness or boredom. She wondered where Harrison was now. She stopped atop a bridge over a small creek bed and leaned over the safety rails and took in the fresh air. The wind blew her long hair behind her. She smiled for a moment at the simplicity of the moment. She felt at peace with herself. Even the perpetual sound of wind chimes that were a result of the wind and weather patterns on the planet did not bother her.

The feeling was not to last long.

She heard many shouts and screams from below and to her left and right. She recognized the sounds of laser rifles and pistols discharging their deadly blasts. Steiner began to crouch down on the bridge and look around her. She saw dozens of families and single individuals running her direction, crying out for others to run for their lives. Others shouted that someone had tried to assassinate the Glorious Leader. She stood up and looked off in the distance at the capital and worried for her friend Siobhan. She was there at the celebration and if there had been an attempt on the life of the Glorious Leader, then what fate had befallen her dear friend.

Steiner's first instinct was to run for the capital and seek out Siobhan. Unfortunately the screaming crowd cut off her only logical route to that destination. Steiner realized that the crowd was growing and rapidly approaching the bridge.   To avoid being caught in the crowd, she began to run to her right and get off of the narrow bridge. From behind her she could hear people and Akarzdamedians scream as they were pushed off the bridge to their possible deaths eighty feet below.

Steiner kept running as the sounds of screams and laser fire continued behind her. She observed several tall buildings to her right and made the quick decision to duck inside one of them to escape the charging mob. She ran as fast as her legs could carry her toward the closest building and ran to the plate glass front entrance. The sliding doors did not open for her as she had hoped. She began banging on the glass with her palms as she looked over her shoulder to see that the mob was about thirty feet away from her. She noticed that there were dozens of soldiers in black Class C uniforms and riot helmets that were firing into the sky to force the crowd in her direction.

Suddenly, the sliding doors opened for her and several sets of arms grabbed Steiner and pulled her inside. The sliding doors slid shut behind her just as the screaming crowd began running by. She fought the hands that were holding onto her sweater and looked around. To her surprise, she was surrounded by dozens of Akarzdamedians. She noticed that she was the only human in the lower level of the large building.

"What in the name of the Stars is going on?" Steiner struggled to get free of the aliens. She noted that the first floor of the building was all black, from floor to the thirty foot high ceiling. There were square columns extending from the floor to the ceiling top. Steiner could see that the room was about five thousand square feet and was completely lacking in furniture or lighting. She could only make out some bright silver hand rails that were on the walls all around the room. They were giving off a glow of silver light that kept the room illuminated.

"Calm yourself," one of the yellow skinned Akarzdamedians told her. He was wearing a blue outfit that resembled an ancient Japanese dress with long sleeves and high collar. The clothing had white trim around the top of the collar and there was a white belt around the robe looking outfit. He was not wearing any shoes.

"There was an assassination attempt on your Glorious Leader," a much shorter and stockier red skinned Akarzdamedian said. This one was wearing a similar robe but it was black with a white belt and trim.

"Release her," a solid black Akarzdamedian ordered.

Steiner felt relieved when the other aliens let her arms go. She looked over the gathering of the Akarzdamedians before her. She estimated that there were around several hundred of them, all in different skin colors and sizes. The black on that was approaching her seemed to hold some stature among the others. The Akarzdamedians slowly parted like the Red Sea before Moses as the black alien made his way to her. She noticed that he was wearing a shiny silver robe with a black belt and black trim around the neck and sleeves. Steiner gasped when she saw his face.

"Cla Cuchulain!"

He smiled at her when she said his name. "Julia Steiner of Lauterbrunnen, Switzerland! My dear friend, I am elated to be in your company again!"

Cla Cuchulain gave her a hug as he had learned to do from Marco on the Blood Moon. Steiner hugged him back.

"I have," Steiner began and was cut off by her friend.

"Many questions?" Cla laughed and waived his hand with four fingers at her. "Follow me. We allowed you and only you to see our dwelling here. The other humans will all run past without seeing the structure. I sensed your presence and realized you were in distress. I could not allow any harm to come to you."

Steiner looked back at the front entrance. "So the crowd outside cannot see the building?"

"No, unless we allow it," the short stocky red Akarzdamedian answered.

"Ah, my manners." Cla smiled. "This is my family. We are part of the underground population. Your leader and his minions do not know of our existence. We have our own economy and structure of leadership here under the planetary crust." He motioned toward Steiner to the others and began speaking in Akarzdamedian.

Steiner could not understand a word that he said. She began to wish she had taken the time to learn the Akarzdamedian language from him on the Blood Moon as Marco Andolini had done. All that was certain to Steiner was that he was talking about her as the other aliens were looking in her direction in awe. Some bowed their heads to her as Cla spoke. Others walked to her and touched her arms or her face in a manner that indicated respect or caring. Steiner smiled back at them as her friend continued his speech.

Finally he turned to her, "I told my people how you killed Caine Rosenburg. They all know that he was my captor, my keeper, during the years I was in bondage."

"I see," Steiner kept smiling as the other Akarzdamedians were still touching her and bowing their heads with respect. She surmised that the idea of a human fighting another human in favor of their species was something special to them. It was as if her killing Caine was an act in defense of their people. She had not considered any inter-racial implications when she stabbed the serial killer. She merely took his life so that he would never be able to harm another.

"Come, we have much to discuss as we break bread together." Cla pointed toward the far wall.

Steiner began to follow as Cla began to walk rapidly toward a doorway that was a light silver color. "What do you mean you have your own economy and leadership? What is all this?"

Cla stopped before the door way and it slid open

revealing a bright silver downward spiral staircase. "Underneath the surface is another world. When your people dropped those weapons of mass destruction on us, most of us fled to the places below. No human has ever seen our homes under the surface. You will be the first and only one, unless the others from the Blood Moon ever visit. They will be welcome here, too. You and your friends liberated me from the slavery of the evil Rosenburg family. I am eternally grateful to you for that. I know you have a special heart. You are a jewel among your people. I watched how you cared for the others that were hurt in the battles on the Blood Moon. You have a grand soul inside you, a spirit of goodness and compassion. With you and others like you, our people can co-exist. We can have collaborations that would benefit both species."

Steiner looked down the stairwell and it seemed to have no end at them bottom. The silver of the rails and the stairs stood out with brilliance against the solid black background. "Where does this lead?"

"To the population of the Akarzdamedians that refused to be conquered," Cla said and motioned for her to begin ascending. "Our Queen has spoken to us all in our dreams for the past two centuries. She says that the day is soon coming."

Steiner felt a chill run up her spine from the way he sounded. "What day is that, my friend?"

"The Day of Atonement. The guilty shall be punished. Our people are prepared to rise up and fight for justice and freedom," Cla said slowly. "Our Queen will awaken soon and she will join your Queen to lead a war that will inspire all of humanity to fight. I ask you now to join us, Julia Steiner of Lauterbrunnen. I ask you to help us and find other humans here, on Akarzdamedia, to be ready to take up arms and fight the tyranny of Vladimir Sikorsky."

Steiner shook her head, faced Cla and looked into his eyes. "My friend, I know nothing of a human Queen. We do not have any such titles in our culture."

The red Akarzdamedian shook his head. "Yes, you do. Our Queen Danu tells us that she will join with your Queen and they will fight. She tells us when they begin the war that we are to do the same."

Steiner found herself doubting the aliens. Cla had made some wild statements that contradicted Earth History while they were waiting to be rescued on the Blood Moon. He had told her that it was Sikorsky that had used weapons of mass destruction on Africa and the Middle-East of Old Earth. He had claimed that Sikorsky refused to enter into peace negotiations during the war between their peoples. Steiner never found any proof that his claims could be verified. Now he spoke of a human queen to lead a battle when no such titles were used by humanity.

"My friend, if you say you have heard these things in your dreams, then how can they be trusted or real? It is not that I do not believe you. It is just that we humans have dreams as well, and ours are not reality," Steiner told him calmly. "You understand?"

Cla took her hands in his and gazed into her eyes. "On the Blood Moon, your leader Yuri Gorski and I spoke of the same subject. He told me his mother spoke to him in his dreams. He would wake up and remember her words of encouragement and that she would tell him she was proud of the man he had become. Do you remember that conversation?"

Steiner shuddered as she felt a cold chill go through her body. She swallowed and continued to look into the eyes of the alien. She had been skeptical then and had not changed her mind on the issue. "Yes. I remember him saying that."

He smiled and leaned into her and whispered into her ear. "He can hear her. She is able to reach her son the same way our Queen reaches us. They speak to all of us.

All one must do to hear them is open up your heart and listen. Yuri hears his mother and she is out there, sleeping in some location, somewhere near or far." He released Steiner's hands and motioned with his arms toward the ceiling. "They can reach out to us while they sleep. Their minds and their spirits can journey into our sub consciousness. I had thought it was always a trait of only my species. But Yuri made me realize that you humans have the same ability. Listen for them. They will speak to you, too."

Steiner felt the chill in her body subside and fade away as Cla motioned to the stairwell. He took her left hand in his and smiled at her.

"We can learn so much from one another," Steiner told him. "I would like to learn more about how the dead can communicate with the living from you."

"Yes," he agreed with a large smile. "Follow me to our hidden sanctuary and you will see things that no human has ever been allowed to view. After we have dined and you have been introduced to the others we will discuss which other humans on the surface can join our people and the movement to bring back justice to this planet and the others that humans have occupied. Will you follow me, Julia Steiner of Lauterbrunnen?"

Steiner smiled, "Yes. And, please just call me Julia."

"You can refer to me as Cla." He said to her as he led her onto the winding staircase.

"The people outside. Are they being killed by the soldiers with the Glorious Leader?" Steiner asked as they descended.

"No, they were only herding them away from the main part of the capital." Cla said to her as they took several more steps downward. "The soldiers will start executing my people on the planet surface in retaliation for the assassination attempt. They will blame all of my species and not be able to differentiate between the guilty and the innocent. All they will accomplish by their cruelty is to strengthen our resolve when Queen Danu gives us the direction to lead our kind to war."

Steiner nodded. She had no love for the Glorious Leader or his family. As far as she was concerned, the connection between Sikorsky and the Rosenburg's was too close for her to ignore. "How can I help?"

"I knew that you would join with us," Cla smiled as he led her down the stairs.

CHAPTER TEN

The United Nations Space Command Battle Cruiser *Waterloo* was moving again. Dirk Fenster watched as the scenery in space began to change with the maneuvers of the *Waterloo*. Dirk looked over his shoulder at his sister, Therese. She was awake and sitting on one of the chairs near the far wall and speaking with their tattooed cousin, Frederick.   The three Allen girls had sat around another table away from the Fenster's. Christian Allen would occasionally glare in the direction of Dirk. Her sisters would do the same. It was no secret that the Allen girls hated the Fenster family.

That hatred made any plans of collaboration to escape impractical. Dirk had considered three different avenues to flee the *Waterloo* and attempt to find help. Each of his three scenarios required that the eight hostages work together as one cohesive unit. With the family feud that existed between the Allen's and Fenster's he had concluded all of his plans were doomed to failure. Even if he could convince the Allen women to cooperate with him, Dirk was certain that the well trained crew of the *Waterloo* would simply vaporize whatever escape ship they could commandeer.

Dirk crossed his arms and watched in the distance space and noticed that the *Waterloo* was moving alongside another Battle Cruiser. Dirk strained his eyes to try and determine which ship it was. It was too far off for him to see the painted name on the side. Dirk further observed several shadows on the grey hull of the distant battle cruiser. He was certain that the shadows were from much smaller Raumschiffs and fighter ships flying by the larger craft.

Dirk looked over at the other hostages. They were all young like the rest. Each of the prisoners had changed into the gold colored uniforms left behind by their captors. Brenda Brackenridge was eighteen years old and had been working on her first year at the Academy in the New York Territory. She was a lovely girl except that she had a long nose. She had long dark hair and blue eyes. She was a few inches taller than Dirk and she seemed to be terrified of her situation in that she rarely spoke. Dirk learned from her that she had a boyfriend back on old Earth and that he was from another well to do family.

Her older cousin, Diana Brackenridge, was about the same height and build.   She also had dark hair and blue eyes. She did not have the long nose of her cousin. Diana was studying for her doctorate in computer programming at Vanderbilt University on Old Earth. She was twenty-five years old and seemed to be a bit uncomfortable interacting with others. Dirk compared her personality to other computer students at Clovis Academy. They kept to themselves and were constantly into their own world. Dirk recalled that Jen Staszko used to use the term "socially inept" to describe the computer majors. He found Diana to be very attractive but she seemed to not realize that men would find her desirable. He learned that Diana did not have any men in her life and she seemed to not understand why the question was raised.

The skin tight gold uniform revealed that both of the Brackenridge women had slender bodies with curves in all the right places. Both of them had on expensive jewelry that Junior Sikorsky allowed them to keep on. Diana had a pair of diamond hoop earrings on and a diamond drop necklace. Brenda had a ring on each of her fingers that sported a different metal such as gold, silver, and platinum among others, a diamond tennis bracelet and diamond stud earrings on.

The last of the unfortunate hostages was a man named William Cullen Breckenridge. He was twenty years old and had been studying for a degree in finance when he was abducted from his dormitory room at the Munich Academy. He had wanted to discuss their possible escape when Dirk continuously admonished him that they were all being watched. That had created a heated argument between the Fenster's and the Allen girls which led to the current segregation of the group. Breckenridge was a physically fit young man and handsome. He had indicated that he was training to compete in a decathlon. He considered himself a ladies man and had many options for romance back on Old Earth.

William Breckenridge attempted to flirt with Diana Brackenridge on three occasions but she seemed to not understand the concept of flirtation. She was excited that a man as handsome as Breckenridge would show her so much attention but she was clearly intimidated and did not know how to handle the interaction. On the third try, Breckenridge gave up on the woman and move his attention to Angelica Allen. She seemed far more receptive to his small talk than the other women in the group.

Angelica Allen was nineteen years old and had been a student of weaponry design at her university. She was as pretty as her sister Christian and equally hateful toward the Fenster kids. The last Allen sister was named Esther. She was sixteen years old and stayed close to Christian at all times. Esther said nothing and would glare at the Fenster's with anger. She had also been told many stories by her family not to trust a Fenster. Recognizing the hatred that the Allen's had for him, Dirk decided to ignore them as he continued watching out into space for any clues.

All of the hostages were smart, educated and seemed to be motivated to achieve things in life. That is all of them except Frederick Fenster. He was the oldest in the room and had colorful tattoos all over most of his body. He was skinny and had little muscle tone due to a decade of defiling himself through illegal drug usage and alcohol. He had body piercing jewelry in both nipples, his tongue and lower lip. Dirk recalled that his aunt and uncle were forced to retain the best defense lawyers in Texas to get Cousin Frederick out of several legal issues. The thing that was most frustrating regarding Frederick was that he was brilliant. Had he decided to ever apply himself to some course of action he would have been a success. Instead, he became a rogue and a criminal.

"Why do you keep looking out there?" Frederick demanded. "I haven't seen you in over a year and you have nothing to say to me?"

Dirk looked over to his cousin, "Get a job."

Frederick laughed, "Now you are sounding like grandfather."

Dirk faced his relative, "What is it that you want me to talk about?"

"Chicks, man. Babes. Women." Frederick leaned back in his chair and looked over the three Allen girls. "I say we all get naked and have an orgy, man. Right here and now. Its good odds for us, Dirk. Six girls and three guys."

"You are a pig," Christian Allen told Frederick. "One of us six chicks happens to be your cousin."

Frederick looked across his table at Therese. "Last I saw you, you were just sprouting. Look at you now. Mmmm. Mmmmm. Yeah, I would do you without a second thought. You really filled out."

Therese stood up and walked over to her brother's side. "Shut up, Fred. You are a pig. At least I can agree with an Allen on that point."

Frederick shrugged. "I was just saying maybe we should keep it in the family, my sweet little cousin."

"She said to shut up!" Dirk yelled at his cousin.

He laughed. "Woooo. Defending your little sister.

How knightly of you, Dirk."

"Will anything shut him up?" Angelica Allen pointed at Frederick.

He smiled at her, "You could, baby. Come over here and get on our knees and..."

"Enough!" Dirk yelled before his cousin could finish the sentence.

"Okay, man, it's all cool. I was just thinking since we are all gonna die that we could have some fun together." Frederick looked away from them all.

"Are we all really going to die?" Brenda Brackenridge asked nervously.

"Not if I can help it." William Breckenridge told her. "Look. All our families have money and resources. They will be looking for us and they will find us. We just wait this out. The Glorious Leader will wipe out these revolutionaries and we will all get to go home soon. We just need to relax and we will be fine."

"No we won't," Dirk faced them all. "My cousin is right. They may keep some of the girls alive for breeding purposes. The Royal's like having multiple wives and creating many offspring. But for the three of us?" He pointed at his cousin and Breckenridge. "We males are nothing but shark bait."

"But I am only sixteen," Esther protested. "I don't want children. Not now, anyway. Why is this happening to us?"

Christian put her hand on her shoulder. "Esther, just stay calm and we will all be fine. And don't listen to any Fenster. Those three are probably involved in this somehow."

Dirk turned away from the Allen's and put his arm around his sister's shoulders. He whispered into her ear. "Terri, I plan on taking this ship."

Therese hid her reaction from the hidden cameras in the room and leaned her head against his chest. "How are we going to do that?"

"I can fly this ship. You can work her engine room." Dirk whispered back. "Remember that father said that two competent people could safely control a battle cruiser. But we need to get to the life sciences section of the ship."

"And gas the rest of the crew?" Therese felt as if she were reading her brother's thoughts. "And then I run the engine room while you pilot from the Command Station?"

"Exactly," Dirk said as he kissed his younger sister on the cheek.

"I am ready, Dirk. I would rather die trying to take over than waiting to be executed."

"That's my little sister. You really are a good Gorski Gang member."

She smiled at him with pride that he would tell her such a compliment.

"What are you two whispering about?" Frederick demanded.

"Nothing," Dirk told him.

Frederick stood up and walked over toward the Brackenridge girls. "How about you two? I will rock your worlds. How about a threesome?"

"Are you insane?" Brenda Brackenridge asked as she pulled her arm out of his reach.

"Okay, so sex is out. For now." Frederick sat down next to Diana. "You two girls got to keep your jewelry. Did they let you keep any red dust or pot, man? I vote we all get stoned."

"We have no drugs," Diana crossed her arms and glared at him.

"Anyone else?" Frederick began walking in circles. His hands were starting to shake from the effects of withdrawals. "Man, I really need a hit, man. Did they leave us a stash, man? Anything? Come on, what kind of hosts are these people?"

Dirk and his sister continued to watch the other Battle Cruiser in the distance. It was not moving.

"Strange. The Waterloo is moving but the other one out there is not." Dirk was silent for a few moments. "If we are being deployed why is that one staying dormant?"

"Maybe she was not ordered out?" Therese speculated.

"Or maybe she is part of the civil war Junior Sikorsky was referring to." Dirk nodded to himself. "Maybe an attack on Sikorsky's Planet is about to happen."

"If that were true, Dirk, then wouldn't they be firing on us right now?" Therese concluded.

Dirk did not have an answer for his sister. He shook his head.

The main entrance to their living quarters slid open. The eight hostages stood up and watched as Junior Sikorsky stormed into the room with five armed MI officers. Sikorsky was now wearing a black uniform with five silver stars on his lapel and a long purple cape flowing from his neck to his ankles. He was clapping as he entered and waited until the doors closed.

"Everyone is comfortable, yes?" Sikorsky asked. "Need anything?"

Frederick raised his left hand in the air. "Sir, may I have some synthetic cocaine or red dust? Man, I am in bad need of a hit."

Sikorsky glared at the drug starved Fenster. The tone of his voice indicated his disdain for illegal drugs. "No, you may not. Now, I wanted to tell all of you that the Second Fleet is out there."

All of their eyes watched as Sikorsky pointed out toward space. He nodded to them.

Christian Allen ran to the observation windows and gazed at the Battle Cruiser in the distance. "Is that them? Is that the Amistad? My uncle Bruce is on that ship!"

Sikorsky clapped his hands again. His eyes were looking her over with lust. "Yes. Yes that is the Amistad. You are a smart girl and very beautiful. When this is over I think we can come to certain agreements, you and me."

Christian scowled at him. "What do you mean?"

"I plan on using your healthy body for breeding." Sikorsky told her and walked toward her. She tried to move away from the man but one of the soldiers in black grabbed her shoulders and held her tight. Sikorsky stopped in front of her and ran his right hand through her hair. "You will create splendid children for me. Very soon."

Christian turned her head away from him in disgust.

"So, if that is the Second Fleet out there," Dirk raised his voice at Sikorsky in an attempt to get him away from the girl, "then why are they not attacking us?"

"Because my young man, they cannot see us!" Sikorsky clapped his hands again and turned away from Christian. "When the war begins they will be fighting the five other ships from the First Fleet. But they will not see the sixth ship of the Fleet. That is us. We will attack them from the rear and kill them all!"

"What!" Angelica yelled as she stood up.

"But Uncle Bruce is on one of those ships!" Esther protested.

Christian glared at Sikorsky, "If you harm my uncle I will never breed with you."

Sikorsky laughed for a few seconds before he slapped Christian across the face. The sound of the impact was loud. Her head whipped to her left and then she fell to her knees.

Dirk growled angrily and charged at Sikorsky but one of the soldiers in black tripped him. He went sliding across the floor. Another soldier lifted Dirk up with one hand and threw the cadet across the room. He crashed into another table. Therese screamed as her brother hit the floor with a thud.

"Soon you will all learn that there is no escape from here." Sikorsky said softly. "In a few moments you will all see our planetary first responders engage the Second Fleet. I will have a holographic live feed displayed for you all to watch on the far wall. Once the Second Fleet is in battle, then the First Fleet will attack. Your uncle Bruce will die as well as his whole crew."

Dirk picked himself up off of the floor and slowly stood up on his feet. The soldier that threw him had considerable upper body strength. Dirk felt bruised on his backside. He recalled that Marco Andolini had been assigned to the Second Fleet after graduation. Now, more than ever, Dirk wanted to escape. He desperately wanted to warn Marco and his shipmates to withdraw from the trap that was about to envelope them all.

Sikorsky was laughing loudly as he snapped his fingers. The far wall became a large view screen of the outer space battle grounds. The hostages could clearly make out the five Battle Cruisers of the Second Fleet that were in orbit around Sikorsky's Planet. There were thousands of small Allen Type fighter space craft visible on the screen along with hundreds of Raumschiff.

"They will all die," Sikorsky shrugged as he and his five men walked out of the room.

The metal doors slid shut behind him.

"Uncle Bruce," Christian said softly as she found the location of the *Amistad* on the screen before her. She reached out to touch the ship as if it would somehow bring her closer to her beloved uncle.

"Look!" William Breckenridge pointed to the lower left corner of the screen. They all saw thousands of small fighter ships flying from Sikorsky's Planet toward the Second Fleet.

"They are going to try and weaken the defenses of the Fleet with small fighters," Dirk thought out loud. "And then they will bring in the larger Battle Cruisers to finish them off."

The Allen girls watched in silence as Dirk and Therese sat down at a table to watch the large screen.

Dirk knew that escaping their prison was hopeless. But, if the battle produced a momentary power loss on the *Waterloo*, then the front sliding doors to their cell and their corresponding security mechanisms would be temporarily disabled. If that moment occurred, they had to be ready to force open the doors and make haste for the lower level of the Waterloo and fight to take control of the engine room.

And the controls to the life support generators for the ship.

Dirk whispered to his sister to be ready, just in case. She nodded in agreement. She was ready to fight back against the brutes that had kidnaped them. Dirk smiled at Christian who glared back at him. He was certain that the Allen girls would join them if the opportunity was presented to them. Their love for their uncle clearly transcended their hatred for anyone named Fenster.

CHAPTER ELEVEN

Captain Bruce Allen paced up and down his Command Station with his hands behind his back. The Planetary First Responders would soon engage them in battle. Allen knew that their first opponents would be thousands of small Allen Type Fighters piloted by alien slaves. Most likely Akarzdamedians, Allen thought to himself. To repel the attack of the thousands of slave flown space craft, Allen and Admiral Khan would be forced to use a considerable amount of their weapons resources. They had to use their counter-measures sparingly so that they would have enough to fight back with when the First Fleet finally engaged them.

"Captain," Gee interrupted his thoughts. "On the main view screen. They are coming."

Allen looked at the three dimensional screen and saw that over three thousand single fighter ships were approaching at full speed to intercept the Battle Cruisers that were part of the blockade. Allen sighed.

"Patch me in to all of our fighters," Allen ordered.

Marco Andolini heard his on board computer warn that three thousand fifty-seven Allen Type Fighter Space craft were on an intercept course with the Fleet. He contacted Benson. "It's on now."

"I know. My computer just warned me," Benson said softly.

"You realize that most of those ships have slave pilots. The real challenge will be coming soon after." Marco told her. "I love you girl. Please be careful."

"I love you too," Benson smiled as she said it. She checked her safety harness around her shoulders and mid-section. Out of nervousness she made sure her enviro-suit helmet was secured. She wanted to stretch her legs as she had been in her pilot's seat for three hours. She saw real combat on the Blood Moon and had no doubt that she was ready to fight and meet the enemy head on. But the other pilots that were in her squadron were relatively inexperienced.   She had given them many pep talks to build up their confidence. The time for words was over.

The war was about to begin in earnest.

Benson, Marco and the other four thousand pilots that were going through similar thoughts of how to fight heard the words of their Captain.

"This is Captain Allen. We will be unleashing the drones and the explosive magnetic space mines in five minutes. They will deploy past you and create a temporary barrier between us and the approaching enemy. The mines should put a big crunch on their numbers. After the mines launch, we will send in our drones to face their drones. Be mindful that all of the drones are equipped with self-destruct capability with an explosive radius of a quarter of a kilometer. So don't get to close to them. After the drones are launched, they will send in their fighter pilots from the Planetary Defense and the fleet. That is when the battle will truly begin. When you engage them in combat, remember to stay with your wing person. Never abandon them. They are your best friend in battle. I wanted each of you to know that I am so proud of you all. To fight for freedom and for liberty for others is the most honorable act any human can take on. If we stick together, then this day shall be ours! If we stand together as one, we can repel these agents of slavery and lies! Will you fight?"

All of the crew members of the five battle Cruisers screamed in unison with the pilots in the small Allen Type Fighters the word "Yes!"

"Then may the Stars guide you!" Allen told them.

Benson was silent as she watched her on board

screen show that the enemy was now under fifty kilometers away.   Marco swallowed and gripped his half-moon steering mechanism and he did his sixth weapons check in three hours.   He did so more out of apprehension of the coming battle than anything.

Marco's on board computer warned that the magnetic space mines were sailing over his ship at full speed. The mines would soon activate and their magnetic component would attach to the metal of the enemy ships and then explode. The mines were about the size of a soccer ball but packed enough explosive force to annihilate a small space craft. He remembered what his friend Porfirio Cardenas always told him. Have faith. Marco breathed easier as he took some solace in the fact that the drone ships and the magnetic mines would be the first part of the battle. It was always the same, the drones would nullify each other, with any luck, leaving neither fleet with any advantage.

Marco heard a female voice in his head that sounded so soothing and almost musical in tone: "I am with you."

Marco was startled by the voice. "Ellen, did you say something?"

"No, why?" Benson's response was quizzical.

"Nothing, I just thought I heard you say something."   Marco looked out the transparent metal cockpit of his fighter ship and only saw ships from his squadron nearby. The binary suns were in the far distance. He dismissed from his mind the voice and began to wonder if it was the same voice he heard on the Blood Moon just before his ship had been destroyed.

The long, slender, silver and black drone ships engaged the drones sent by the Planetary Defense forces of Sikorsky's Planet. In the distance, Marco observed as the microchip computer operated drones fired rockets and lasers at each other, littering space with metallic debris as they exploded. The drone portion of the battle ended as Marco had assumed it would. Neither side was left with an advantage over the other. Within forty minutes, all of the drone ships were destroyed.

Marco watched in the distance of space as the magnetic space mines began to activate and were drawn to the metal hulls of the enemy space craft. They began to attach and enemy ships began exploding in deep space. The fireballs of the explosions were short lived due to the lack of oxygen to support the fire. But the metal wreckage of each destroyed enemy ship spiraled in different directions. Marco felt badly that the mines were killing many slave pilots. He recalled the Akarzdamedian he had befriended on the Blood Moon, Cla Cuchulain. Once Cla had been freed from the microchip that controlled him he proved to be helpful and a good side kick for as short as it had lasted. Marco prayed that Cla was not among the Akarzdamedians that were now dying. Marco thought he could see hundreds of ships exploding in the distance. The display would temporarily brighten the darkness of space and then slowly return to the void that surrounded them.

But the mines did not intercept all of the enemy ships. Many were still on course to engage Marco and the other pilots. He asked his computer to give him an estimate of how many enemy space craft were left. His computer responded by telling him that there were over two thousand eight hundred combatants flying toward them.

Marco instructed his squadron to stand ready. "When they get in range, and not a second before, fire your first armor piercing rocket."

Lieutenant Junior Grade Ezra Tulley acknowledged Marco's order. He could tell by her voice that she was scared. Marco felt that his mouth was dry from fear as well. He told Tulley to take in some deep breaths and calm herself.   "Are they in range?" Marco asked as he could see on his monitor that some of the enemy fighters were getting closer.

"Fifteen seconds," his computer answered.

"Lock Missile One on my opposite opponent." Marco instructed the computer.   "Launch in fifteen seconds."

To Marco, the next fifteen seconds felt like an eternity. He heard his computer announce that his first missile had launched. He also heard that the enemy ships had launched their missiles as well.

Over six thousand Allen Fighter Type space craft began a deadly dance in the middle of space, in between Sikorsky's Planet and her binary suns. Humans in the Eight Solar Systems were able to watch the battle live due to the numerous satellite system throughout the vast reaches of space. Some humans were cheering on the forces of the Glorious Leader. Others for the ships that supported Admiral Khan. On Cootron, Admiral Cardenas watched the events from the conquered governmental skyscraper palace room along with many of his friends and co-conspirators. On Earth those that had advocated changing the government watched and dared not breathe. Everyone that were following the speeches of Brey Gillis in Dublin understood that if Khan could hold on and succeed then it would spark insurrection around the Eight Solar Systems. It was critical that the blockade stand so that the rest of humanity would be encouraged to fight for regime change.

"Evasive action!" Marco ordered his squadron as he began to pull his controls upward to guide his ship in a northerly direction. As he began to increase his speed he could see to his right that his squadron was following him as he had previously instructed them to do. He heard his computer inform him that his first missile scored a direct hit and the alien ship was destroyed.

All around Marco were ships spiraling past at high rates of speed. There were numerous ships exploding from laser and rocket hits. Some of the explosions occurred close in proximity to his position and he felt the concussions rock his ship back and forth. Marco quickly asked his computer to keep him informed of any losses on his squadron. He fired a few laser bursts at some enemy ships in the distance and noted that one of his targets spun out of control and collided with another ship. Both exploded on impact.

Marco pulled his ship around to face the enemy and fired his second rocket. His squadron copied his action and each pilot fired another missile. The alien ships were swarming all around them now and individual space craft were now engaging each other one on one. He could hear an occasional death cry from one of the pilots from his side. Marco forced his ship forward and began firing his lasers at two enemy ships that were closing in on him head on. One of the ships erupted in a ball of fire and metal as he scored a direct hit. The second ship was peppered with laser blasts from Marco and went spiraling out of control when some of his laser shots ripped through the transparent metal cockpit and sliced into the unfortunate Akarzdamedian pilot.

Marco observed that there were just over a dozen enemy ships flying toward Benson's squadron, which was already outnumbered. Marco yelled an order to his squadron to fire upon the ships to support Benson and her pilots. In seconds the enemy ships that were attempting flank Benson and her team were obliterated.

Benson had her squadron taking a more aggressive position in the battle. After the first volley of armor piercing missiles had been launched, Benson ordered her squadron to fly directly at the enemy and rain down a hail of laser fire on them. Benson had eight kills in just under thirty seconds of the battle. Her bold leadership against the enemy was precisely why they targeted her and her squadron. By the time Marco and his squadron began protecting their flank, Benson had twelve kills. She fired her lasers with deadly accuracy and continued to blow enemy space craft to pieces.

All around the squadrons led by Marco and Benson were ships chasing one another and shooting lasers and rockets. Many ships would explode around them. The entire battle moved quickly as neither side would break off the attack. Many Akarzdamedian slaves died in massive explosions of flesh and metal.

Captain Bruce Allen noticed from his Command Station that several enemy ships had broken through and were flying directly at the Battle Cruisers. His three dimensional display revealed that the ship commanded by Del Rey was firing lasers at the approaching ships and blowing them to pieces.

"Lieutenant, order weapons section to begin picking off the enemy that is approaching. And please instruct them to be careful. I don't want any of our ships hit by friendly fire." Allen ordered as he paced in front of the three dimensional views of the vast battle before him and smiled. His side was winning a decisive victory. The ships that were sent from Sikorsky's Planet, although superior in design and manufacture, were no competition for pilots that were fighting for freedom.

In the weapons section of the *Rorke's Drift*, Dia Cho was seated in one of the two dozen laser canon weapons and was firing at approaching enemy ships that had gotten past the fighter ships. Cho had trained in the Academy on the proper use of the weapon. The laser canon had been designed and constructed by the engineers from the Fenster Corporation eighteen years ago. It had a barrel that extended out twelve feet and had a two foot wide radius and was connected to a six foot tall rectangular metal backing that kept the barrel upright. Behind the backing was a leather seat that had laser sightings so that the operator could accurately aim at approaching targets. Operating the weapon took skill as it fired a laser blast that caused a kick back that was fifty times more powerful than the average laser rifle. The operator had to learn to fire the laser weapon in a manner that would lead the moving target.

Cho was a master at that art. She calmly watched the computerized targeting screen before her and held a black detonator in her hand that she would simply squeeze to activate the firing mechanism. She had on headphones over her ears to hear them order coming from the Command Station and to drown out the noise of the other weapons being fired around her.

She fired at several ships and her lasers were annihilating everything she targeted. She had lost count after the sixth small Allen Type Fighter ship that she had blown up. To her left were several Technical Sergeants seated in similar laser canons. They had also been firing and destroying approaching enemy vessels. The entire team in the weapons section took pride in the knowledge that their Battle Cruiser had not been grazed by an enemy directed laser or rocket.

Felicia Essex helped the weapons technicians with reloading the armor piercing rocket launchers. During battle the technicians had to move quickly so that the ship could stay fully armed and fend off attack.

Marco kept pressing the laser trigger on the front of his steering column. Ship after ship exploded before him due to his accuracy with the laser controls. He had been keeping count of his kills during the battle. But at some point he lost count. He kept firing and swerving his ship to avoid lasers and rockets that were being fired at him. Soon everything grew quiet.

"Cease firing!" Lieutenant White ordered.

Marco and Benson both released their fingers from their laser controls and surveyed the vastness of outer space around them. All of the enemy attackers were dead. They had succeeded in repelling the first wave of attack from the Glorious Leader.

"We did it!" Dell screamed in joy.

There was mass applause. Marco tried to raise Benson and finally got through to her.

"Baby, are you okay?" Benson asked over her communication system.

"Better than okay. You?"

"Marco it was unbelievable. Even the simulators cannot prepare you for the actual feeling of combat. According to my computer I shot down nineteen. And I feel terrible for each one."

Marco removed his helmet and sat it in his lap. "I know how you feel. It was war, but I feel sick to my stomach that I had to kill those Akarzdamedians. They all deserved a better fate than that."

"It is not what I expected when I was studying at the Academy," Benson mumbled.

"Hey, Ellen. When this is over, I want to take you to New Edinburgh to meet my parents and the rest of the family." Marco said, mainly to change the subject.

"I would like that."

"I want you to meet my twin, Dominic. You would really like him. His wife, Harumi, is a sweet girl and you two would get along great."

"I hope we both live through this so you can take

me to meet them all. I really want you to meet my family, too."

"We will get through this," Marco said hopefully. "We will make it."

In the weapons section of the Battle Cruiser *Rorke's Drift*, Dia Cho and Felicia Essex hugged and kissed as the rest of their weapons technicians did the same. One of the Garrisons had been helping them in the battle and hugged Cho and Essex, congratulating both women for being courageous warriors. Neither woman had expected the victory to be so one sided, but it gave them hope that soon they would be returning to the moon called Robert Andrews and retrieving their children.

The entire ship erupted in cheers of jubilation due to the fast and decisive victory. Captain Del Rey smiled for a few moments and allowed her crew to celebrate and hug for a while. She knew that the Glorious Leader would be sending in more ships against them. She dreaded the thought of Admiral Perdicas and his First Fleet. They were the best of the best.

Admiral Khan relaxed for a few moments as well as he sat in the Captain's seat on the *Montenegro*. He, like Del Rey, knew that the First Fleet was the best in the Space Command. Khan also knew that Perdicas and his military experts sent in the three thousand plus fighter ships to die so that they could study the tactics of the enemy. Now Perdicas knew how each squadron behaved in combat. He would instruct the next set of enemy pilots accordingly. Khan was certain that the next battle would not go as easy as this one had.

On board the *Waterloo*, the hostages watched the battle on the three dimensional screen that Junior Sikorsky provided for them. Christian Allen hugged her sisters as they were cheering on their uncle Bruce throughout the melee.

Dirk Fenster began to realize that the victory for the rebel pilots had been far too easy. He did not want to verbalize his fears that the Glorious Leader and his commanders were testing Admiral Khan's tactics. They sacrificed a few thousand ships and pilots to study their fighting styles. Dirk shook his head at his sister and she nodded that she understood what he was thinking.

The celebration of the victory by the crew members of the Second Fleet would not last long.

Renee Starr approached her sister, Jayne and smiled at her. All of the pilots on board the flagship of the First Fleet were treated to a large three dimensional view of the battle on the roof of the Docking Bay. Many of the pilots were stunned that their allies were wiped out so quickly.

"You see, Renee?" Jayne whispered. "They came to fight. They will not back down."

"But it is our duty to fight for the Glorious Leader," Renee whispered back.

"For all we know the Royal family was the reason our little brother Roy got killed. What did the Royal's ever do for us? Think about it, Renee. Think about it long and hard. Are you willing to go out there and die like those other pilots just did? That was a slaughter."

Renee crossed her arms and looked down at the metallic floor of the Docking Bay. For the first time in her life she did not know what to do. "Sis. What should we do when we get the order to attack them? I mean, is this really a war we should be involved in?"

Jayne hugged her sister and whispered into her ear. "Shhhh. Be careful with your words. The MI officers on this ships have ears everywhere. When we are sent out to fight we will do so. But we need to look for the first opportunity to get away. Our little fighter ships have a long range, we can get out of the solar system before the solar cells drain. By then we can find a place to hide out until this is over. You with me?"

"You always were the smartest one of us."

Jayne kept her arms around her sister and whispered into her ear: "Then stay with me and do as I tell you."

As the sisters continued to hold each other they heard the voice of their commander, Admiral Perdicas. "Attention all pilots! You will launch in ten minutes to engage the enemy. Weapons section personnel are on red alert as of this moment. We are going to face the Second Fleet in all-out war. This is a fight to the death. The Glorious Leader will be watching our every move and will hope for our success. We must make him proud! Happy hunting!"

Renee Starr wrapped her arms around her sister. "We are really going to do this?"

"Just keep your communication lines open and listen for my cue. When I tell you, follow me and we will get to a safe place."

"Okay."

"Now go. Get on your ship, and Renee, watch your back."

Captain Trent Janssen was sitting patiently in his Captain's seat on the Command Station of the Battle Cruiser *Remagen*. He waited as Marine Corps Colonel Aldo Ortega and his Executive Officer, Lieutenant Commander Shauna Gannon walked over to meet with him. Admiral Perdicas was standing behind Janssen's chair.

"So, what did you observe?" Janssen asked Ortega and Gannon.

"The pilots that faced ours are a little bit inexperienced," Gannon stated. "But they stood their ground and fought. They did not panic at all. If we are going to defeat and kill all of them pursuant to the orders of the Glorious Leader, we will have to break their spirits."

Ortega nodded in agreement, "I also noticed that the squadrons are loyal to each other. Some of the pilots would break off to defend another squadron that was outnumbered. They also used their armor piercing rockets sparingly. Our opponents seem to have a preference for laser to laser dog fights."

"And what does that suggest to you?" Perdicas cut in.

"It tells me that these pilots are brave and have a high confidence in their individual and collective abilities." Ortega directed his response to the Admiral.

Perdicas nodded in agreement, "We will break their backs as Shauna suggested. Tell our Battle Cruisers to arm their rocket launchers with several armor piercing nuclear warheads. Instruct the Waterloo to move in behind Captain Allen's ship. We will destroy Khan's Battle Cruisers with nuclear weapons and then let our smaller fighter ships hunt down the survivors. Send out word that we are ordered to kill them all. No prisoners of war will be tolerated by the Glorious Leader. Hunt each and every one of them down and kill them. And we need to let the rest of the Eight Solar Systems know that we killed them all. This is not just about this battle. Other planets are beginning to demand regime change. If we crush Khan and Allen decisively then it will create a chilling effect on anyone else thinking they can stand up to our family. Plus, without Khan or Allen, they will be lacking in leaders that have experience in space warfare. Therefore, they must be eliminated first. Concentrate everything on the ships led by Khan and Allen."

"Agreed," Janssen said.

"Kill them all," Perdicas repeated his order.

Marco and Benson received their orders from Captain Allen to conduct a roll call. Benson learned that two of her pilots from her squadron had died in the battle. Marco reported in that he lost one pilot, Patricia Dwyer. He barely knew Dwyer although she had been his shipmate for several months. She had been quiet and kept to herself other than the time she had sex with another crew man in front of everyone. He hoped the woman did not suffer.

"The First Fleet is moving in," Captain Allen warned all of his pilots and the other Battle Cruisers. "This time we aren't just facing single fighter ships. They are launching Raumschiffs and the five Battle Cruisers are coming to join them. This is it. You all need to fight like a starving animal looking for a meal. May the Stars be with each of you."

Allen turned his attention to his Command crew. "Notify the other Captains and let them know that the enemy Battle Cruisers are coming straight at us. Battle Stations!"

CHAPTER TWELVE

Marco looked over his computer screen display and cursed when he saw that each of the five Battle cruisers of the First Fleet had launched eight hundred Allen Type Fighters from their Docking Bays. He confirmed that there were fifty Raumschiff space craft launched from each of the enemy ships. His screens showed an additional three thousand Allen Type Fighters approaching from the surface of Sikorsky's Planet. Marco placed his helmet back on and secured it.

"Four thousand from the Battle Cruisers and three thousand from the surface," Marco said to himself. "That would mean we are outnumbered over two to one. Well, the Academy brochures did promise action and adventure."

Marco told his on board computer to conduct a weapons check and to patch him into his squadron. "All ships, look alive. We have boogies approaching from north, south, east and west. By my calculations we are outnumbered by two point five to one. I once fought twenty-four against four and lived to tell about it. We stick together and keep our cool, we can survive this. Stand with me."

Benson took in a deep breath as she fidgeted in her seat inside her Allen Fighter Type space craft. She had calculated the numbers and the odds just as Marco had done. She checked her weapons and was confident she had enough laser charges to sustain a long fight. She waited for the orders to engage from either Admiral Khan or Captain Allen.

Captain Allen had taken a few moments to excuse himself to his personal quarters. He ordered Lieutenant Gee to arrange a conference-com discussion with the commanders of the other ships in the fleet. Allen did not have to wait too long as he saw the three dimensional red colored images of Khan, Del Rey, Harvard and Rogers.

"Perdicas has us out gunned," Allen stated the obvious. "I recommend that we unleash all of our remaining magnetic mines to make the fight fairer."

"But what if they send in even more ships on a third attack?" Harvard asked. "If we use all of the mines then we will be wide open."

Khan shook his head side to side. "No. We need to play this like it is the last attack. Bruce is correct. We need to deploy all of the mines. If we can push back their small fighters and Raumschiffs then we can advance on their Battle Cruisers. We need to take the offensive. If we play this too conservative we could lose too many pilots. Unleash the mines and I also recommend that we start dropping the titanium rods on the military targets located on the planet surface below."

"If we are going to fight this as the end game battle, then should we use the timed explosives also?" Del Rey suggested. "We could launch them now and detonate them when they get near the Battle Cruisers. If we get lucky enough to hit one it could harm their morale."

"So ordered," Khan agreed. "I know we all had hoped that Sikorsky would voluntarily step down. He didn't. We also had hoped that other commanders would join our effort. They did not. We are alone and outnumbered. If things start going badly for us in the next few hours, and you feel you need to withdraw to save your ship and crew, then do so. Perdicas is not going to take prisoners. We stand and fight but withdraw if we need to. Everyone understand me?"

All of the four commanders nodded.

"Let's give them hell," Allen said softly.

He watched as each of his co-conspirators slowly

faded away. He quickly walked from his quarters back to his Command Station and to his fate. Allen motioned for his crew to carry on when they stood to attention for him. None of them knew that it would be the last time they would do so.

Unseen by the Second Fleet, the Battle Cruiser *Waterloo* was maneuvered into position behind Captain Allen's ship.

As Allen's weapons technicians were launching their magnetic mines and titanium rods, the Waterloo weapons section began to prepare to fire weapons far more destructive. Junior Sikorsky supervised the crew of one thousand nine hundred men and women prepare for war. He had held back his eight hundred fighter pilots since the presence of the *Waterloo* would have been detected had he launched them. Sikorsky waited until he could eliminate the Battle Cruiser under command of the savvy Captain Allen to break the spirit of the traitors.

Sikorsky walked down stairs from his command Station to the weapons section on the second level of the *Waterloo.* He observed in silence as three hundred men and women began loading armor piercing nuclear warheads into the rocket tubes. He could tell that they were ready to reveal themselves to the enemy. All he needed now was the word from Admiral Perdicas to fire the weapons of mass destruction at the enemy. Sikorsky was wearing a gold silk bathrobe with black slippers and gold silk pants. He never considered his eccentric choice of clothing as strange or odd. He was the son of the Glorious Leader and wanted to stand out among the rest of the crew.

Satisfied that his crew had their weapons ready for attack, Sikorsky decided to roam to the third level where his hostages were being held. He had taken a strong liking to the attractive Christian Allen. He was certain that over time she would understand why her uncle had to die. And when she came to that logical point of enlightenment, she would be able to love him and breed with him with great passion. Sikorsky traveled without his children, grandchildren, wives and other family members just in case he had the opportunity to court a new love interest. And he certainly coveted Allen.

Sikorsky arrived on the third level and motioned for the ten guards with solid black uniforms to follow him inside the prison cell. As the sliding doors opened for him, Sikorsky walked in clapping his hands together as was his habit. He had watched his father clap his hands often and picked up the trait himself. He smiled when he saw the three Allen girls sitting together at one of the tables, holding hands and watching the three dimensional view of the looming battle. The Allen girls looked at Sikorsky and his guards as they walked in.

Dirk and Therese had been standing next to the large observation window, watching the Battle Cruiser of Captain Allen and the Allen Type Fighter space craft that were preparing to meet their opponents in combat. Dirk moved in front of his sister in a protective manner. Frederick was curled up on the floor with his arms wrapped around his torso, shaking from the effects of his withdrawals and sweating profusely. The Breckenridge and Brackenridge children simply glared at Sikorsky and his guards as they stormed in.

Sikorsky smiled at them all, "My dear guests! The end is near. I just received word that Admiral Weems and Admiral Cardenas have been eliminated. Now we shall watch as Admiral Khan dies."

"Sir, with all due respect, my cousin needs medical attention." Therese pointed at the corner of the room where he was lying on the ground. "Can't you help him out?"

Sikorsky scratched his head and walked over to the prone Frederick Fenster. "Get up!"

Frederick did not respond.

"I said get up!"

Dirk cleared his throat, "Sir, he cannot get up. He is going through some serious withdrawals. He was hooked on Red Dust and synthetic cocaine for years. We sent him to numerous rehab facilities back on Old Earth and he would start reusing in no time. He needs some pain killers to get him through this."

Sikorsky growled and turned away from the tattooed Fenster and faced the other two. "And what about you two? Are you also using Red Dust? How do I know that the whole lot of you aren't a bunch of stupid spoiled rich kids that use drugs every day?"

"No sir, we never did such things!" Diana Brackenridge protested.

Sikorsky realized that he had been diverted from his real mission when he saw Christian sitting at the table. She was so lovely to him. He had to have her for himself.

"My dear Christian Allen!" Sikorsky forgot the Fenster family and walked over to her. "I think it is time that we became more, shall we say, friendly. I suggest you come with me and watch the war from my suite."

"Never," Christian glared at him.

"Never is such a long time and so full of finality. I could be good to you."

"You want to be good to me? Then let me and my

sisters go home. Surrender to my uncle Bruce and do everything he is asking. Then maybe we will talk."

Sikorsky sighed, "Yes, of course. You are playing the old game of mouse and cat with me? Hard to get as they used to say in the west? Well, my dear, I am sorry. Because in just a few moments this war will be over. Your uncle is going to be dead in a few minutes. Old Earth will be wiped out. Cootron and Athena will have every living human reduced to dust. It is over. If you were smart, my dear, you would recognize that you should be nicer to me. I hold the keys that will determine who in this room dies and who lives."

Brenda gasped when she saw that Frederick was struggling to his feet. He was dripping with sweat and his legs and arms were shaking as he used the wall to balance himself upright.

"So you are not as bad off from all of your illegal narcotics after all?" Sikorsky clapped his hands.

"I prefer the term hyper potent psychedelic synthetics," Frederick struggled to get the words out. "And that girl, Christian, she's mine fatso. So stay away from her."

Sikorsky grimaced at the offensive remark over his slight stomach bulge. "Did you just insult me?"

"Damn straight."

Sikorsky looked over at two of his guards, "Teach him some manners."

The two guards quickly moved in on Frederick and knocked him to the floor. While he was on the ground they began kicking him in the side and in the face. Therese tried to intervene but another guard slapped her in the face, sending in her sliding on the floor. Dirk also jumped in and got in two punches in the side of one of the guards that had been kicking Frederick. It took two guards to restrain Dirk as he kicked and struggled to free himself.

"Enough!" Sikorsky called off the guards. He stood over the beaten Fenster and gloated. "You drug infested loser! You can never have a woman like her. I am the one in power which means I get the woman and you get crapped on! Remember that!"

Angelica Allen had gone to the aid of Therese and was helping the girl to her feet. Diana Brackenridge walked carefully past Sikorsky to assist Frederick.

"You are all so ungrateful to the wonderful hospitality I have provided you. I will contemplate this when Old Earth is gone and each of you have no use to us any longer. Let's leave these gnats and watch the war from the Command Station!" Sikorsky led his guards outside.

The sliding doors sealed after the last of them had left.

Before leaving, the two guards restraining Dirk tossed him to the ground. As he looked up at the large three dimensional display he saw how the chess pieces were being placed on the outer space battle field.

"The attack is about to begin," Dirk said as he stood up. "Your uncle is outnumbered."

"He is smarter," Esther assured them.

"I hope so," Dirk said thinking of Marco.

Marco noted that the magnetic mines had been launched from the five Battle Cruisers and were sailing over their position in the direction of the over three thousand slave operated ships in the distance. Behind those ships were the fighter ships that had been launched from the Battle Cruisers of the First Fleet. Behind those were the rapidly approaching five Battle Cruisers from the First Fleet.

Marco and all of the other squadron commanders continually urged their pilots to hold their positions. They waited for the mines to detonate.

But they did not.

The mines sailed past the small space ships being flown by the slave Akarzdamedians and continued toward the second wave of ships.

Admiral Perdicas gave his staff a confused look. "Did they malfunction?"

"They figured it out," Ortega said. "The first wave is the slaves. Our pawns. They are going to activate the mines over our better pilots. They are trying to take out our bishops and rooks."

Perdicas grunted, "Khan is too damn smart for his own good."

Ortega was correct in his observation. The magnetic mines were activated over the force of ships closest to the First Fleet. They began to attach to many ships and explode, destroying ship and pilot in a brilliant eruption.

Jayne Starr pulled her fighter ship downward and narrowly avoided one of the mines that was sailing toward her. She heard her wing man scream just as his ship collided with one of the round objects. His death cry lasted only a split second before his ship was torn to small fragments. Jayne began calling for her sister as she heard more of her fellow pilots cry out just before they died. To her relief, Renee Starr responded that she had not been hit.

Jayne estimated that they had lost over one thousand pilots due to the mine attack. She could hear Captain Janssen urging them to attack and wipe out the traitors. She began urging her squadron to reform behind her ship and follow her lead into the battle.

Marco ordered his squadron to fire a round of armor piercing rockets at the incoming ships. He noticed that all of the squadrons were doing the same. A large number of the slave operated ships were destroyed in that volley. The space battle had begun. Marco flew his ship directly at the enemy, firing wildly at them. His pilots did the same. Ships were exploding all around them. Marco heard his wing woman scream as she was hit by a rocket. She died instantly when her ship erupted. Marco saw the explosion out of the corner of his eyes.

Captain Allen ordered his weapons section to fire upon the military targets on Sikorsky's Planet. He could see that the battle was progressing well for his side. They had made major dents in the disparity of the numbers. He hoped that the trend would continue.

Captain Constance Jared of the *Waterloo* looked to her weapons officer on the command Station. "Commander Sikorsky? We are in range. Please have your staff in the weapons section deliver the first defeat of the day."

Jared was eighty years old but looked not one day over thirty. She was a Royal descendant and took full advantage of new skin and body parts from the lower income level humans. She had positioned her ship just behind the *Amistad* and had all of her rocket tubes loaded with armor piercing nuclear weapons. Her voice sounded like a monotone and she never smiled. To her, killing the lower class citizens was like another day dawning. It was all routine.

Her second in command and weapons chief was Commander Josef Sikorsky. He was a great grandson of the Glorious Leader and known to be ruthless. He smiled when Jared gave him the order and passed the order on to his section. The technicians in the Weapons Section of the *Waterloo* obeyed and fired five nuclear warheads at the Amistad. At that same time, Captain Jared ordered her pilots to pull the *Waterloo* back out of range so that the explosion would not damage their ship.

Captain Allen heard the warning klaxons on the Amistad that there were incoming missiles locked onto his ship. With a look of confusion on his face, he looked to his crew members on the Command Station. "Where the hell did they get fired from?"

"From our rear, sir!" Gee sounded panicked.

"Sir," the hybrid wolf-human weapons technician named Lox looked at Allen with fear in her eyes. "Those weapons are nuclear and they are armed."

Allen stood up and felt as if he was going to throw up. "ETA to impact?"

"Ten seconds!" Gee responded.

"Alert the crew to brace for impact!" Allen yelled over the constant blaring klaxons. He wondered how other men and women reacted knowing that they only had seconds to live. His last thoughts were on what his life could have been had Iridia lived. He wondered what their children would have looked like. He closed his eyes and tried to remember her face on the first night they met, the color of her eyes, the whiteness of her teeth when she smiled at him.

And then his life was over.

The nuclear warheads slammed into the hull of the engine level and weapons level of the *Amistad*. The warheads easily cracked through the metal of the *Amistad* and the missiles slammed into the walls. Several engineering and weapons technicians were sucked out into outer space from the hull breaches. The rest of the crew soon joined them in death. All five of the nuclear missiles detonated simultaneously.

The fabled UNSC Battle Cruiser *Amistad* erupted in a brilliant flash from the five nuclear explosions. Captain

Allen and his crew were dead instantly. The ship was torn to small fragments of metal from the power of the explosions. The nuclear eruption was brilliant and the colors were enhanced by the darkness of the surrounding outer space. Some of the pilots around the doomed ship died as they, along with their smaller fighter ships, were annihilated.

Captain Jared knew that five missiles were overkill. But she wanted the rest of the eight solar systems to see the massive explosion. She wanted them all to witness that death would be the result if they dared challenge the Royal family. The force of the explosion caused many of the closest smaller fighter ships to vaporize when the nuclear blast hit them. Most of the victims of the reach of the nuclear explosion had been fighter ships from the *Amistad*.

Marco and Benson had led their squadrons deep into the battle and were untouched by the explosion. Their on board computers warned them that the *Amistad* had been destroyed. Marco was surrounded by enemy fighters and had no time to react to the news. He was in the fight of his life. He fired laser bursts at many moving targets. Ships flew by him from his right and his left. He hit some and missed others. He was weaving his ship left and right to avoid lasers fired at him. Benson was experiencing the same stress level. She fired and kept firing. The numbers of the enemy ships around them were supreme.

Dirk Fenster and the other prisoners on the *Waterloo* witnessed the destruction of the *Amistad* from their prison room. The three Allen women were beside themselves with grief at the death of their beloved uncle. Esther kept mumbling that Captain Allen had never forgotten to send her gifts on her birthdays as she wept. Christian was sobbing over the death but said nothing. Dirk prayed that Marco Andolini would be smart enough to escape.

Admiral Perdicas pressed his advantage. He ordered his other ships, the *Tanaka*, the *Vasco de Gama*, the *Dag Hamaskjold* and the *Arizona* to target the other Battle Cruisers from the Second Fleet. Each of the First Fleet Battle Cruiser's fired nuclear warheads at their targets.

Admiral Khan was stunned at the loss of his friend and his flagship. He ordered that the remaining ships return fire with nuclear weapons. He had not wanted to use such powerful offensive devices as he had hoped that the other side would cease the battle once the smaller fighters of the Second Fleet won the day. He cursed himself for having been so naive in thinking that the Glorious Leader might fight with any kind of honor or dignity. He ordered his chief pilot to bring the Battle Cruiser around ninety degrees so that they could have a clearer shot at the lead Battle Cruiser of the First Fleet. But he did not have time to maneuver his ship into position. The Admiral and his crew aboard the UNSC Battle Cruiser *Montenegro* perished when seven nuclear weapons slammed into his Battle Cruiser. Khan cried out to the other three commanders to withdraw from the battle. He was dead before Harvard, Rogers or Del Rey could respond to his desperate orders.

The Battle Cruiser was ripped to pieces by the explosion. Just as with the destruction of the *Amistad*, many smaller fighters were caught in the nuclear explosion and were annihilated. Other pilots that had been looking directly at the *Montenegro* when it erupted were blinded by the nuclear flash. Without their eyesight, those pilots became easy kills for their opponents. Within the span of ten minutes, Khan and Allen were dead and their Battle Cruisers destroyed. The effect on the morale of the remainder of the Second Fleet was interesting to Perdicas. He had specifically targeted their ships first due to his belief that the other ships would cut and run once Khan and Allen perished. They did not. The smaller Allen Fighters and Raumschiffs continued to fight on. Perdicas speculated draconian order of the Glorious Leader to kill them all might have been the reason that they fought on.

Del Rey saw both of her dear friends die on her screen. She thought she heard Khan's last command to be an order to withdraw. She directed some of her tactical technicians to scan the area nearby the *Amistad*'s destruction. One of her officers noticed that the stars just behind the location where the *Amistad* had once been were being obscured by a large mass.

"Another ship. How did it become invisible?" Del Rey asked out loud. "And how many more are there?"

"Ma'am!" one of the computer technicians yelled over the sounds of the weapons fire and chatter from the space craft fighting to the death. "Lieutenant Rogers on screen for you!"

"What is going on?" She asked as she received the communication from Lieutenant Rogers.

"Dana!" Rogers yelled from her command post on board the *New Delhi*. The stress on her face was evident. She had blood on her forehead from a gash she received when she fell into a panel during the battle. "We need to withdraw! There is an invisible ship out there! We are now outnumbered two to one on Battle Cruiser strength. Our fighter pilots are good but we need to get them and the rest of us to safety!"

"I agree!" Del Rey yelled just as she felt the floor beneath her rippling from an explosion. Del Rey was thrown violently to the ground and watched helplessly as many of her tactical and computer technicians were thrown from the upper balconies to the lower level. Several died from the fall. Others were lucky enough to suffer only broken bones. Del Rey noticed that one of the Love-Easter Replicants was lying on the floor, his body twisted in an awkward manner and his eyes wide open. She concluded he had fallen from one of the balconies and died in the fall.

The computer began sounding warning klaxons of hull breaches in the engine section and the living quarters. Del Rey picked herself up with the assistance of one of the Garrison Replicants and demanded a report.

"Captain!" One of the engineering officers on the third level balcony of the Command Station called out to her. "An enemy Raumschiff collided with us and ruptured the hull on impact. Everyone in the engine room was killed! The engine is irreparably damaged. The dunkle materie converter is destroyed! We are losing power!"

Del Rey turned her attention back to Rogers on her screen. "Go! Save as many as you can! We are finished here. I will have to beg for mercy from Admiral Perdicas."

"You mean leave you?" Rogers demanded with strong emotion in her voice.

She never received an answer. Rogers and her crew were vaporized as three nuclear warheads destroyed her Battle Cruiser. Del Rey covered her eyes due to the brilliance of the bright flash on the screen from the explosion. Rogers had been her friend for many years and felt sick that she was gone. There was nothing left of the *New Delhi* and her brave crew of just under three hundred. Del Rey ran to her chair and demanded that a communication channel with Admiral Perdicas be opened immediately. Del Rey cursed as she made her way to the seat and silently wondered why they had never learned that the technology had been developed to cause an entire Battle Cruiser to become invisible. If that were possible, then what other advanced weapons or technological advancements had the Glorious Leader kept secret?

She prayed that Harvard and her crew were able to escape the slaughter.

Gloria Harvard recognized that the day was lost. She sent out a distress call to all of the remaining Allen Type Fighter ships and Raumschiffs to follow her Battle Cruiser at full speed away from the binary star solar system. She hoped that she could attract the attention of the

First Fleet Battle Cruisers long enough to give some of the pilots the opportunity to escape safely. Harvard yelled to her weapons section to return fire at all of the First Fleet Battle Cruisers. Her crew performed admirably. The world watched through live satellite broadcast as one Battle Cruiser stood against five. Harvard and her crew rejoiced when one of their armor piercing rockets made a direct hit on the Battle Cruiser *Vasco de Gama*. One of Harvard's tactical officers informed her that the hit was to the engine room of the enemy ship. Harvard could see the *Vasco de Gama* begin to drift in space as she no longer had any power.

"Keep firing!" Harvard encouraged her crew.

Admiral Perdicas was calm in his seat on board the flagship of the *Arizona.* His pilots skillfully flew the Battle Cruiser through the dozens of enemy fighter ships and Raumschiff to position her just behind the *Nigeria.* They were in range. The crew waited for his command. Perdicas paused for a few dramatic moments.

"Weapons section, are the nuclear warheads armed?" Perdicas asked.

"Affirmative, Admiral."

Perdicas licked his lips, "Fire five nuclear warheads into the Nigeria. Once launched, move us out of range at full speed."

His crew followed their orders and launched the missiles.

While *Harvard* and her crew were firing on the *Vasco de Gama*, they had lost sight of the *Arizona*. *Harvard* had assessed the odds. If they could get past the *Vasco de Gama* and her small fighters, they might be able to get out into the open space outside of the war zone and escape.

But the UNSC Battle Cruiser *Nigeria* was doomed. The fact that the *Arizona* was able to flank her and fire several nuclear warheads at her weapons area was not expected. *Harvard* and her crew heard the dreaded warning klaxons from their computer system that warned them impact was imminent. One of her tacticians on the third balcony informed her of the number of missiles that were approaching. *Harvard* put on her safety harness and smiled at her stupidity. She knew a nuclear explosion would vaporize her body in seconds. It was pointless. She had her computer patch her into the rest of her crew. She wondered what words she could say that would comfort her crew, knowing that they were all about to die. She concluded that there were no words that mattered. There was nothing that she could think of to tell her crew that their deaths were not in vain. None of the other fleets had made efforts to support them. They were going to die and their deaths would be for naught.

"This is Captain Gloria Harvard. I wanted you each to know that it was an honor to be your commander. If you have a God, now would be the time to make peace with her. I send my apologies to the rest of humanity that we failed today. Best wishes to all."

Harvard had much more to say but the nuclear strike from the *Arizona* cut her short. She had wanted to send a message to her father, mother and numerous siblings to explain her actions. Her last thought was that she should have taken care of that after they rounded the moon Robert Andrews. The *Nigeria* was obliterated by the nuclear blasts and all of three hundred eighty crew members were vaporized in the explosion.

The *Rorke's Drift* was hit by several more rockets causing damage to the weapons section and the medical area. One of the rockets exploded in the area where Dia Cho was working her laser canon to fend off the attacking Raumschiffs and small Allen Type Fighters. She felt her machine rock with the explosion. She could hear screams from her fellow crew members as they died from the blast. Cho tried to keep firing her laser canon but it had been rendered inoperable from the explosions. She realized she had a massive gash in her left leg from some flying shrapnel. Cho climbed from her post and surveyed the scene of devastation around her. She could hear the safety bulkheads closing to stop the loss of oxygen from the hull breach. The laser canon to her left was burning. She could see the burning body of Technical Sergeant Carria Woods strapped in the machine. Through the flames, Cho observed three large pieces of metal that had embedded into Woods body. Cho felt sympathy for the woman as they had become friends over the few years that they knew one another. During their time on the *Rorke's Drift*, everyone had agreed that Woods had the best hair of the crew. Now her hair was burned away and her once lovely face and figure were ravaged by shrapnel and fire.

There were small fires all around the weapons section. Dead crew members littered the floor. Many had limbs severed. Some of the bodies were burning. Cho saw about a dozen weapons technicians trying desperately to load more rockets into the launch tubes. There were many wounded as well. Technical Sergeant Jiannaha Jordan was lying on the ground clutching her abdomen where a large piece of metal was imbedded. Cho saw that there was another piece of metal sticking out of Jordan's left eye. Jordan seemed oblivious to the wound to her eye as she moaned in agony on the metal floor.

Through the carnage and destruction, Cho could not find her wife, Felicia Essex. She began to scream for her over the sounds of fire and grinding metal. Cho heard her call to her from behind a pile of metal that had once been a wall separating the commander's offices from the main weapons storage.

Cho limped in the direction of Essex's voice and saw her on the floor, pinned under torn metal. The pieces of the metal had Essex trapped to her stomach. She had blood on her mouth and was coughing. Her face had several cuts from flying metal shards and glass. Cho ran to her and grabbed her outstretched left hand.

"Felicia! Hang on! I will get you some help!"

"Dia," Essex said with her eyes rolling around. "I can't see. I can't see anything! I can't feel my legs."

"Hold my hand my love!" Cho pleaded. She wept at the sight of the love of her life trapped under the metal. "I love you so much, Felicia. Please hold on while we get medical up here."

"I love you, too. Dia. I know I am dying."

"Don't say that Felicia!"

"No, it is okay. I was loved, Dia. You made living worth it. Our children made my life with you something I would never trade. Leave me, Dia. Try and get a ship and get out while you can." She coughed out blood in between her last two sentences. She tried to focus on Cho, to see her one last time, but her injuries had been severe enough to cost her eyesight.

Cho gripped her hand tighter as Essex was struggling for each precious breath of air. The end would come for her soon. Cho determined that her place was at her side. She would not leave her to die alone.

On the Command Station, Del Rey finally received an open holographic communication line with Admiral Perdicas. She had only one hope, to plead for mercy with a man that had already demonstrated he possessed a heart of stone.

"Admiral, this is pilot Dana Del Rey of the Rorke's Drift. I wish to discuss terms of surrender with you." She paused and saw no reaction at all on Perdicas' face. "My engine room is destroyed. My weapons section can no longer mount a defense. I understand that my life as the Captain of this ship is forfeit. But I plead to you to spare my crew. Please. We offer total and complete surrender to you, sir."

Perdicas considered his personal feelings regarding his next words due to his love for any man or woman that signed up to serve in the military. He wanted with all his heart to show mercy to the crew of that ship that had fought so valiantly. But he was a Royal Family member first and he had no choice as his father had given the order that all of the treasonous Second Fleet had to die. "I am sorry, Captain Del Rey. The price of treason is death. Tell your crew that I am launching on you now. I estimate that each of you have about thirty seconds to make peace with whatever deity soothes you."

"Admiral!" Del Rey shouted over the sound of fire and sobs of the wounded. "Please! Show mercy! We are beaten! There are good people on this ship! You don't have to do this!"

Del Rey felt a warm tear running down her right cheek as she heard Perdicas instruct his crew to fire. The klaxons had been damaged by some of the other rocket fire and could no longer warn of potential danger to the *Rorke's Drift*. Del Rey swallowed and wiped the tear away.

She asked her ship computer to patch her into the survivors of her ship. With her voice wavering with emotion, Del Rey did her best to tell her fellow crew members' good bye. "This is your Captain speaking. Several nuclear warheads are on their way and we will all be dead in about fifteen seconds. I wanted to say good bye to each of you and thank you for your service. You were the best crew I could have ever hoped for."

Dia Cho held the hand of her lover tight as she braced for the nuclear explosion. Essex pleaded with her to try and escape. Cho told her she loved her and kissed her lips. As the women kissed the nuclear missiles slammed into the hull of the *Rorke's Drift*. Cho and Essex died holding hands with their lips locked in an eternal showing of their love. The explosion was bright and when it subsided, the *Rorke's Drift* and her crew were gone.

Throughout the eight solar systems there were audiences that watched the massacre from the safety of their homes or space stations or ships. The message was clear: No matter who you are or where you come from, turn on the Royal Family and you will die.

Jayne Starr had lost about half her squadron in the main battle and was speechless as each of the Battle Cruisers of the Second Fleet were vaporized by the nuclear explosions. She had ordered the squadron of her sister to combine with hers. Renee Starr's squadron commander had been killed as had her second in command. Renee was more than happy to become older sister Jayne's wing woman. They watched as patches of small fighter type ships from the destroyed Battle Cruisers flee in different directions. They had no mother ship to return to and were lost.

Jayne felt that as fellow pilots the best thing to do was allow the vanquished to flee. But it was not to be. She and the remaining fighters from the First Fleet received new orders from Admiral Perdicas.

"All fighters. Seek and destroy all of the stragglers from the Second Fleet. Kill them all and don't return to base until you do. The victory must be complete."

Jayne bit her lower lip and opened her communication channels to her squadron, "We have been ordered to pursue and kill the remaining Allen Type Fighter ships from the Second Fleet. I noticed that a cluster of them were flying toward the binary stars to our three o'clock. Form a V formation on my ship. We will pursue at full speed. Our orders are to kill them all. No prisoners."

Jayne wondered who the unfortunate survivors were. She hoped that none of them had been classmates of hers at the Academy. She had shot down twelve ships in the battle and had grown weary of all the killing. She took hold of her half-moon steering column and forced it forward to get her ship flying at full speed. The sooner they took care of business, the better.

The final battle between the Second and First Fleet was essentially over. All that was left was to clean up of the mess.

CHAPTER THIRTEEN

Marco Andolini had destroyed over forty enemy ships in the two separate battles. He had watched in horror as all five of the Battle Cruisers of the Second Fleet were annihilated by nuclear weapons. Marco had studied little military history in his days as a student at Clovis Academy. In all of those lectures he attended and papers he read and researched, he learned enough to know that the war was over. His first thought would have been to surrender, but Del Rey had attempted that and was murdered by a nuclear onslaught. So the only way to survive was to escape to a planetary system that might be sympathetic to the cause or go somewhere to establish a new identity on some uncharted location.

Marco ordered that the remainder of his squadron form on him so that he could lead them toward the other side of the binary stars to the east of his position. In his mind, that was the safest direction to flee. The First Fleet were still orbiting Sikorsky's Planet and no other ships had arrived to assist in the effort to kill off the survivors. That left only the pursuing Allen Type Fighters of the First Fleet to be worried about.

Marco attempted numerous contacts with Ellen Benson. After his fifth try she responded to him.

"Marco!"

"Ellen, thank God you are alive. Can you make it to the far side of the binary stars?"

"Yes, I think so. Things are hot where I am right now! Most of my squadron is gone." Marco could hear the sound of rapid laser fire as she spoke to him.

"Just meet me there, Ellen! From that point we will decide where to go!"

"Love you!" Benson terminated the conversation as she fired at a cluster of fighter ships from the First Fleet. Like Marco, Benson had shot down over forty ships. She may have even broke fifty kills in the two combined battles. She had lost count and no longer cared. Her only hope was to rendezvous with Marco on the other side of the two stars and escape the draconian edict of the Glorious Leader.

Lieutenant Targa Jara White had done her share during the battle. She had fired her armor piercing rockets at the Battle Cruiser Arizona and had scored three direct hits.   That was just before the first nuclear explosion occurred which startled her enough to get away from the large Battle Cruiser. She had notched over fifty kills in the two outer space clashes. She noticed that there were a few dozen surviving ships flying at full speed toward the binary stars in the far distance.   She barked an order to the remaining pilots under her command to follow the others. She knew that would be the safest place to regroup and plan their flight to some location that would offer them all asylum.   Many other survivors were flying in different directions as they attempted to avoid the laser bursts from the enemy space craft.

White acknowledged her on board computer giving warnings that there were several hundred Allen Type Fighters in pursuit. She pushed her space craft to reach a speed over five hundred thousand kilometers per hour. She pulled in behind a small group of enemy ships that were behind the remnants of Marco's squadron. White opened fire with her lasers and cut down two enemy space ships. She twisted her ship downward to avoid shrapnel from the two explosions.   She continued her high speed chase to safety.

Marco conducted a role call as he led the last few pilots of his squadron to safety. Ezra Tulley was still alive as was Mary Winston, Azalia Dell, Newton Soto, Eferalia Iduna and Roberta Largo. That was all that remained from his forty-two pilots. Marco felt as if he had failed. Only seven astronauts were left from his first command. That meant that thirty-five pilots under his leadership had died.

"Computer, how many fighters are in pursuit?" Marco asked as several laser bursts passed his ship on his left.

"A full squadron," the computer responded.

"What is our current speed?"

"Five hundred sixty thousand kilometers an hour."

"Push it to six hundred thousand."

Marco felt the power boost as his ship picked up speed. He cursed as another set of laser bursts fly overhead. He hated running. He wanted to stand and fight but the forty-two against seven odds were worse than what he had experienced on the Blood Moon.

"Marco!" Tulley yelled. "Some of our own are engaging the squadron pursuing us."

"Who are they?" Marco looked out his transparent metal observation window. He could not see any ships to his north, east or west.

"They have the markings of the Second Fleet," Winston responded.

"We cannot keep running!" Largo added.

"Agreed," Marco barked. "On my command we cut left and flank the enemy. This might be our only chance to escape. So make every shot count!"

"We need to make them pay for killing all of our friends," Dell responded.

"Keep your heads!" Marco instructed them. "Left flank, now!"

Renee Starr was proud to follow her sister Jayne and the rest of the squadron in pursuit of the fleeing traitors. As they chased the seven fighter ships that were fleeing toward the largest of the binary stars they were surprised when Targa Jara White and her remaining space craft attacked them from their right flank. Renee screamed in surprise as the two ships closest to her exploded in a hail of laser fire.   She heard her sister shouting orders for the fighters to take evasive action. There were more explosions around Renee as she pulled her ship hard right to escape the kill zone.

Jayne Starr cursed as she watched the seven ships they were firing upon cut to the left as others attacked her squadron from the right. They were going to get pinned in between them.   Jayne ordered her pilots to take evasive action as she kept firing her lasers at the seven space craft ahead of her. Her flurry of lasers hit one of the seven ships as it was turning left. The ship spun out of control before it exploded.

"We lost Winston!" Dell screamed as she witnessed Mary Winston die in an eruption of fire, metal and flesh.

"Stay together!" Marco ordered. He had one of the enemy ships in his sights and he pressed the laser fire buttons on his steering mechanism. He watched the target he was firing at erupt in a small explosion of flesh and metal. He heard another scream over his communication system as another of his pilots died. Marco was now firmly on the left flank of the enemy and he sprayed the pack of ships with laser fire.

Marco could see that White and her fighter ships were fighting like hellions against the superior numbers. Ships were being blown to pieces on both sides.

Jayne recognized that the group she had elected to pursue were extremely talented pilots and combatants. She fired her lasers over and over again as she led her surviving pilots away from the wedge the opposition had put them in. She urged her pilots to split in two to face the flanks and fight back. The other fighters from the First Fleet were too far off to be of any assistance as they had been following the ships that were fleeing in opposite directions. Jayne and her ships were on their own.

Renee swerved her ship to the right and was pressing her firing button before any enemy ships were in her direction. She was firing due to the adrenaline flowing through her and causing her to be a bit jittery. When her ship finally faced the ships to her right, she hit two blowing them into slivers of metal. She felt her ship shake from the concussion of the ship to her right exploding from an armor piercing rocket hitting it head on. Renee heard her computer warning that some shrapnel from the other craft had caused some minor hull breeches in her own ship. She took in a deep breath as she fired again on another target.

Jayne kept pressing her pilots to fight as she fired on another enemy ship. In the distance she could see several other survivors of the Second Fleet approaching from the west. The situation for her and her remaining pilots was quickly becoming untenable. They were about to be squeezed from three different fronts. The only direction left for them to go was the same area that the traitors were going.

Toward the largest of the binary stars.

Renee received the order from her sister to make best speed toward the largest star. She pulled her steering column to guide her ship upward. She fired another laser burst and ripped another ship apart as she escaped the conflict.

White smiled as the pursuers quickly became the prey. She ordered her remaining pilots to give chase.

Marco gave a similar order to his remaining squadron members. His computer reported that Winston and Largo were dead. The rest were following him in pursuit of the enemy fighter ships.

The speeds reached in the pursuit reached over seven hundred thousand kilometer an hour. Marco and White led what was left of their squadrons, a mere eleven ships, as they followed the remainder of the enemy ships that had once stalked them. To Marco's pleasant surprise, the fighter ships that joined them were a rag tag group of six ships led by Ellen Benson.

"Marco, it was hell back there," Benson told him as she steered her space craft to come alongside his. "We lost a lot of good pilots, but we made the pilots of the First Fleet pay. We shot down five of their ships for every one of ours."

Marco smiled at that, "That's my girl. We need to keep pouring it on the ships ahead. Their commander is the most skilled pilot we have faced in the last two days. He or she won't go away easy."

"The largest sun is so big up close," Benson observed.

"The heat coming from it is intense," Soto added.

"Everyone keep your enviro-suits on," White warned them. She had taken advanced training on safely flying by stars that emitted high temperatures and one of the recommendations was that a sealed enviro-suit would keep the heat level down. "The opposition is flying around the sun to the back side. Let's keep on them!"

"What about that invisible Battle Cruiser?" Dell asked.

"If it is here, we would be able to see its mass in front of the sun," Marco told them. "It may be invisible, but it has mass and that cannot be hidden. Look out for a large dark spot in front of the sun or the other stars and that will be your invisible ship. The darkness of space will hide it. The bright stars and sunlight will make it visible by casting a shadow or showing its image to us."

"The enemy ships are rounding the sun!" Benson warned.

"Follow them!" White ordered.

Unfortunately for the pilots following White, Jayne Starr was a far better and more experienced strategist. As

Jayne led her pilots around the curve of the large sun she ordered them to come about so that they would be facing their adversaries. Jayne's plan was to fire upon the enemy as they rounded the sun and take back the advantage from them. She ordered her pilots to have their lasers ready. As soon as the other pilots came around and into view they were to open fire.

They did not have long to wait.

Four of the ships came into view and were quickly blasted into scrap metal by Jayne and her pilots. Marco cursed as he watched the space craft in front of his explode. Benson let out a string of expletives as well. White cursed herself for being a fool for not seeing that move coming. She screamed out an order for the others to take evasive action and to fire back. Her voice was shrill and sounded as if the stress of the situation had finally gotten to her.

Marco fired blindly as he pulled up just seconds before he flew into the spot of the doomed pilot that had been in front of him. He exhaled as several laser bursts passed just under his ship. He could see the enemy in the distance and he forced the nose of his ship to face them and he opened fire. He hit one of the ships near the middle of the pack and watched as the unfortunate pilot perished when the space craft was torn in two. The ship did not explode, but it slowly began to fall toward the sun below. Marco had hit the engines and caused it to lose power and thus the gravity of the sun was drawing the ship downward.

Benson also scored a hit when she faced the remaining enemy ships. The explosion of metal and flesh was hardly noticeable in front of the bright sun below.

Several space craft erupted due to the fire fight.

Jayne Starr yelled for her remaining pilots to head north. She fired one last burst and took out another member of the opposition before she pulled up on her steering column to avoid the remaining few approaching ships. She flew north and within seconds she saw them.

"By the Stars!" Jayne Starr gasped.

"I see them, sis!" Renee yelled. "What are they? They look like flying skyscraper buildings!"

In their view were eleven of the two thousand foot long Red Javelin's that were slowly orbiting the large sun. Unknown to the few remaining pilots on either side, these were the weapons that Professor O'Connell had launched into space for use when the time came.

Marco, Benson, White, Dell, Soto and Tulley brought their space craft to a complete halt. They were the only six left alive. In the distance there were four of their enemies left. Ten ships that had been locked in a battle to the death and now confronted with something that they had never seen before.

Or so they thought.

Benson quickly asked her on board computer to analyze the craft before her. "They are exact duplicates of the weapon that was used to kill all life on the moon Chronos."

Benson ordered her computer to send that information to the remaining pilots with her.

"My God," Marco said softly. "Eleven of those world killers? What in the name of all that is holy is the Glorious Leader planning to do with them?"

Jayne Starr ran a similar scan of the eleven monstrous structures in the distance as Benson had. She shared the results with her sister and the last pilot on their side named Shea Lau.

"They are world killers," Jayne said to the others.

"What do we do?" Her sister sounded exhausted.

The elder Starr contemplated their next move. They were outnumbered by the opposition. But they seemed to have little desire to continue the fight. Perhaps everyone had grown weary of all the death from the past day. She was certain the other pilots were as exhausted as hers were. Jayne asked her computer to see if it could intercept any and all broadcasts from Sikorsky's Planet regarding orders from the Glorious Leader.

Marco and Ellen had done the same.

The pilots did not have to wait long before their computers began to play a live speech from Vladimir Sikorsky. All of the nine remaining combatants listened to every word of the man that had turned them into adversaries.

Sikorsky had ordered that his public relations team carve out a thirty minute time spot on all of the major broadcasts through satellite and computers. He wanted all of the eight solar systems to hear his words and to feel the dread of the certain death that would soon follow. The people of Earth were watching the floating broadcast screens in the sky as Sikorsky began his speech.

"Ladies and gentlemen!" Sikorsky waived his arms outward as he smiled to the cameras. He was wearing a long black cape with a white double breasted suit and black tie. His hair was neatly combed, not a strand out of place. For two hundred years he had perfected the art of public speaking and convincing others with his words.

"I bid you a good day. Our union is strong my loyal citizens. We have just successfully repelled and killed all of the rebels from the Second Fleet."

"Hmmph," Benson said to herself. "We're still alive out here asshole."

"I survived a cowardly assassination attempt last night," Sikorsky continued as he smiled broadly. "I can assure each of you that I was not hit by the Akarzdamedian killers. I have issued martial law for Sikorsky's Planet to round up each and every Akarzdamedian for interrogation. We must determine who was involved. But this planet is not the only one that has been in need of a stronger military presence.

"I have sent in the Lysander to planet New Edinburgh to replace the traitorous leaders there. The reports I have received indicate that those that had not followed the will of this government have been arrested and removed from power!"

There was a roar of applause from pre-recorded audio of a crowd from another speech. The Glorious Leader was actually speaking before several cameras without an audience present. But his propaganda machine would add in shots of fake crowds cheering him on for the effect of swaying public opinion.

Sikorsky used his hands to act like he was wishing for the fake crowd to cease the applause so that he could continue his speech. He waited for dramatic effect before he continued with the speech.

"I have been informed that planet Cootron has declared independence from our United Nations!" This statement was followed by a loud chorus of boos. Sikorsky waived at the imaginary crowd so that he could continue. "The settlement on the moon named Robert Andrews have stormed the military buildings, assassinated the Royal Family members there and declared independence!"

There were more jeers from the taped audience to sway the listeners. "On Old Earth, the Nevada Territory, Ireland and Eastern Europe have declared independence." This statement was followed by more of the loud recordings of the fake booing. When the recording began to subside, Sikorsky continued his speech. "Planets Rycon, Nestor, Felder, New Sao Paolo, New Quebec, New Seattle, New Bangkok and New Moscow have all declared for independence. The situation is unacceptable. I have convened my Security Council and the following Resolution and Declaration has been issued. We have authorized the use of the Red Javelin Weapon, the same that was used to punish the traitors on the moon Chronos, to be fired upon the eleven planets and satellites that have turned their backs on the rest of us!"

Those that were watching were treated to more applause and clapping for the announcement.

Sikorsky smiled and waved to the fake crowd. The cheers began to decrease in volume as he spoke some more. "To preserve the eight solar systems all on those rebellious worlds shall be vaporized! We shall be able to populate those worlds with people loyal to us and our government!"

The applause was deafening. Marco had to ask his computer to decrease the volume. "He is so full of shit."

Jayne Starr bit her bottom lip. The man she had been willing to die for, that she had fought for and killed for was going to murder over forty billion people. She had not been on New Edinburgh when her little brother Roy died. She did not understand why Roy did what he did, rushing in to defend others against the odds. For the first time, she understood Roy. She looked at the eleven ominous weapons in the distance and she sighed. "We have to stop this."

"I have ordered my weapons experts to deploy eleven Red Javelin Weapons and detonate them over the rebellious planets and moon," Sikorsky continued. "While we understand that over forty billion men, women and children will die, we also know that by their deaths we grow stronger! Those that are not loyal to this government must be eliminated! The universe is not a safe place! We have enemies everywhere! If any planet is allowed to leave our government it will only encourage our enemies! Today, the Red Javelin's will launch! Within the next few weeks, all life on the rebellious worlds will be extinguished!"

There was more applause that erupted from the recordings controlled by the public relations experts.

"Soon we shall be stronger! Soon we shall be unbeatable! None shall stand against us! All hail the Glorious Leader! I love all of my loyal subjects! I love you! Peace and prosperity to humanity!" Sikorsky was yelling as politicians in the past to be heard over the applause. He waived and blew kisses at the cameras as his image faded away.

Jayne Starr watched the six enemy ships that were facing her three. Only nine ships and eleven Red Javelins. She knew that there was no choice. They had to join the survivors of the Second Fleet to destroy those weapons.

Sitting in his seat, Marco came to the same conclusion. "Computer, scan those weapons and give me an analysis. Can they be destroyed?"

Benson asked her computer the same question. She could not stand by and allow billions of innocent people to die.

Marco contacted White, "Lieutenant, did you hear the speech?"

"Of course I heard it," White responded. She had been contemplating giving the order to fire on the three enemies across the darkness from them.

"I think we should try to talk to them."

"Talk to who?" White asked.

"Those three fighter ships from the First Fleet. We have them outnumbered and they might be willing to listen to reason."

"What the hell for?" White demanded.

"To see if we have any common ground with them. They may have family or friends on the eleven worlds the Glorious Leader just ordered annihilated," Marco responded. "They sure don't seem to be in any hurry to start fighting again."

"That's because we outnumber them two to one."

"And while I appreciate that, they would probably kill three of us before we got them if we engage them," Marco said calmly. "Let me at least try."

White was grinding her teeth. She wanted to blast the last three ships and get to Robert Andrews moon and scoop up her husband and children before the Red Javelin got there. "Fine. Talk to them."

Marco ignored the tone of voice he heard from White. He asked his computer to open a communication line with the three opposing ships. He waited until the computer indicated that he was connected. Marco cleared his throat. "I don't know any of you. I am Marco Andolini. My parents brought my brother and I from Italy on Old Earth to a planet named New Edinburgh. I play futbol. I was pretty good at it. But I wanted to speak with you about a possible truce. The speech from the Glorious Leader is precisely why my friends and I joined the insurrection. Those weapons over to the rear of your position are about to kill billions of people. Maybe someone you know is in harm's way. I want to destroy those Red Javelins. I want you three to help me do it. If you don't care about all those other people, just say so and we can finish this battle between us. You can cut in and answer any time."

Marco went silent as he waited for a response.

Renee Starr remembered him from the Clovis Academy. He had been in the Gorski Gang while she was in the Bragg Gang. His words made sense to her in that the weapons had to be stopped. She wanted to say something to her sister before she responded to Marco. After a few seconds of silence she concluded that any truce was a treasonous act and she did not want to expose Jayne to potential prosecution. She finally decided to act alone and responded. "Marco, this is Renee. Renee Starr. You and I had a few fights back in the day."

Jayne Starr had her computer give her a complete breakdown on Marco's background. He had been one of the Blood Moon heroes. He had also been one of the cadets that stood up to the Ragnarsson assassins when Roy Starr was killed. She shook her head and smiled. "What are the odds?"

"Renee Starr?" Marco laughed. "Really? So our space battle is just like old times. I always wondered what had happened to you after you had graduated. I am sorry about what happened to Roy and Bill."

"Thank you. I felt badly for your friends that died on the Blood Moon," Renee told him. "Were any of the other gang members with you?"

"Dia Cho and Felicia Essex were on one of the Battle Cruisers. The nuclear assault from your side took care of them. I had many friends on those ships in addition to Dia and Felicia."

"I am sorry for your loss," she said. "Look, my sister Jayne is here. I will butt out of the conversation while you speak with her. But I wanted you to know that if you want to blast those Javelin weapons, I am with you."

With full understanding that her words would be punishable by death, Jayne made the decision to accept the truce that Marco had offered. "Mr. Andolini, my name is Jayne Starr and I am in agreement that the nine of us can cease hostilities. I also agree that we have a much larger issue with the imminent destruction of several population centers. I have heard of your words Marco and I understand that you are a man of your word. I will join you in your mission to destroy the Red Javelin's."

"Me, too!" Renee blurted out. "We have to do something."

Benson had listened to her lover as he continued to negotiate with the enemy. Her computer notified her that it had completed scanning the schematics of the Red Javelin. It had several recommendations. "Computer, broadcast your findings to the other eight space ships."

"The Javelin weapons are vulnerable on the rear where the exhaust and burned fuel exit. Each of the weapons have four large rear exhausts that if you were to fire lasers at a close distance, then you could cause the weapon to explode. There is just one problem."

"And that is?" Benson raised her eyebrows.

"If you cause the destruction of a Red Javelin it will explode with enough energy to match several nuclear explosions."

White cut in: "If we fire on them and make a direct hit, what are our chances of survival? Can we outrun the explosion?"

The computer was silent for a few seconds. Finally it answered the question. "The chances of surviving are less than five percent."

The nine pilots were silent as they each pondered their own mortality. Benson rubbed her stomach. She wanted to live long enough to give birth to her child. But forty billion people versus nine made the decision for her. "I don't care. I'm in."

Marco nodded as Benson spoke. He knew she would not back down. She had demonstrated amazing courage on the Blood Moon and would do so now. "I am, too. We cannot let those weapons reach their destinations."

"I am in," Jayne affirmed.

"Count me in sis," Renee said softly. She swallowed hard, thinking of all the things she would miss when she was dead.

"I'm in," Soto said. His father was a Representative in the General Assembly of the UN on planet New

Edinburgh. But his grandfather was the Secretary General of the Security Council on planet Rycon. His aunts and uncles were living on Rycon as well as many of his cousins. Rycon had been terra formed a century earlier and had grown to a one of the largest population centers for humanity. The planet had twice the land mass as Old Earth and triple the water. Although Soto's father had left Rycon to seek opportunity on New Edinburgh, he still thought of Rycon as his home. He had even returned to that planet to attend the Academy there as opposed to Clovis Academy on New Edinburgh. He was certain that his relatives would be involved in the overthrow of the government on Rycon.

"Me too," Tulley spoke up.

White was silent. She found the willingness to sacrifice themselves admirable but stupid. She had a husband and children. They needed her and she was going back to them. "I am really sorry, but I am out of here. Attacking those things, that is suicide. I wish the rest of you all the best, but I am cutting out of here."

Dell was silent during all the mutual statements of the others on how they were willing to risk dying. Dell was only twenty-one years old and had no desire to die without living many more years. Since she had no personal stake in the direction of the Red Javelin's she was not able to see how it made sense for her to die in a foolish attempt to destroy them. She had been lucky on several occasions during the conflict with the First Fleet. She escaped certain death eight times in the battles, laser bursts missing her ship by inches and two armor piercing rockets missing her vessel only to claim the life of another pilot. She had survived for a reason and it was not to die blowing up a massive weapon. She was glad to hear that White had some sense. "Sorry, I am with Lieutenant White. I didn't sign up for any of this and just want to go home. I am sorry."

Shea Lau was the last to speak. She had been recently promoted from Lieutenant Junior Grade to Lieutenant. She had been given exemplary scores on her tests and had several positive reports in her personnel file from higher officers. To die out in space like the way the computer was describing was not how she had imagined she would go out. She had been born and raised on planet New Sao Paulo. Her many younger siblings living there with her father and mother. She fought back tears as she thought of her family that had been condemned to death and forty billion lives was something she could not ignore. "Count me in."

Benson felt rage at the fact White and Dell decided

to abandon them. Although she wanted to say something different, she chose her words carefully. "I understand that the two of you feel like you have a lot to live for. So do we. You can't turn your backs on all those people. They need you both."

"Sorry Ellen," White cut her off. Her guilty conscience was already bothering her. She did not want to listen to any of the others trying to talk her out of leaving. She had her computer block all of the communications from the other pilots and opened a direct channel with Dell. "Let's go."

"Sorry guys," Dell said softly as she heard White's command. She felt terrible about leaving the others to die. But she wanted to live. Committing suicide by firing on those weapons of mass destruction was not something she was willing to do.

The remaining seven watched in silence as White and Dell pulled their space craft away from the others. Marco wanted to call out to them as he watched their two ships fly off back toward the large sun. It was clear that White and Dell were going to try and be on the other side of the sun when the Javelin weapons exploded.

"Don't judge them harshly," Jayne Starr told the rest. "Maybe they will be the ones to tell our story to the rest of the world. Shall we begin?"

"Let's do this," Benson answered her.

"Follow my lead," Jayne told the others. "Since there are only seven of us, I say we target the Javelin weapons that are going to the largest populated planets. We might get lucky and cause a chain reaction. But in case we do not, we have to save as many of the people as we can. Let's get these ships flying at top speed!"

"I am scanning the eleven weapons," Benson reported as she began flying her space craft toward the weapons. "They are starting to move. My computer is calculating which Javelin has been programmed to hit those higher population centers. I am sending each of you the results."

"I have a rocket left," Marco reported. "I kept it for a last resort in the battle. I guess I had delusions that I would get close enough to one of those Battle Cruisers and do some damage to it. So, I can hit two of the Javelins. I know you want to go for the highest population centers, but we left all of the children of the Second Fleet on the moon called Robert Andrews. I want to make sure we take the Javelin that is going there out. It's the least we could do for our departed ship mates."

"I agree," Jayne said softly. Those poor children

would all grow up without their parents thanks to the cruelty of the Glorious Leader.

Jayne began to pick up speed to pull in behind the Red Javelin weapons. She locked her laser sightings on the one going toward planet Earth. Benson was locked on the one going to Cootron. Marco locked on the one that was going to wipe out the population on Robert Andrews. Shea, Tulley, Renee Starr and Soto picked their targets.

Each of their space craft was closing in on six hundred thousand kilometers an hour. They were closing in on the giant weapons.

"I think White and Dell had a good idea!" Benson shouted. "When we fire on the weapons we need to fly as fast as possible to the largest sun. We might be able to get protection from the explosions if we get to the other side!"

"Great idea, honey!" Marco yelled. His speed was now reaching six hundred fifty thousand kilometers an hour. "Everyone, once you fire on your target, fly like there is no tomorrow to get to the other side of the star! It might be our best hope!"

All of the pilots were holding their steering columns tight and had their fingers on the laser triggers. Jayne called out to them to fire on her mark. They all watched as the Red Javelin's grew closer and closer to them. The weapons were moving a little bit faster than before, clearly heading to the planet they had been designated to attack.

On Earth and Cootron the people were in a panic. People were rioting and looting in the streets as they knew their end was near. On Robert Andrews, the population was mostly subdued, praying and hoping for miracle. Planets New Quebec and New Sao Paolo were allowing mothers to take their children on the few transport ships available to escape the promise of instant death. The other planets that were targeted were doing the same.

On Earth the leader of the Eastern European Block watched his three dimensional screen in his castle fortress. His several wives were behind him as he looked closer at the image. He had twelve children and over thirty grandchildren sitting around the large brick and stone room. They were all quiet as they comprehended the severity of the event.

They were all going to die. That was something that even the youngest children in the room could comprehend.

Janicek squinted his eyes at the three dimensional screen. He pointed at the seven smaller objects moving in toward the Red Javelin's.

"What are those?" Retired Admiral Janos Janicek

asked his wives. "They look like Allen Type Space fighters. What are they doing?"

Janicek had been one of the highest decorated Admiral's in the Space Command. He had retired several years ago and was impressed to accept the Presidency of the Eastern Europe block of nations. He had not encouraged revolution, but supported it when the people rose up. Although he had his own ships to flee in, he had refused. He told his family that he would be a part of whatever fate the people suffered. He had a large contingent of his children and grandchildren gathered around the three dimensional viewers to watch the launch of what would destroy all life on old Earth. He remembered the frequent dreams of Melita Gorski warning him of pending disaster. He silently wondered if the Red Javelin weapons were what she was warning him about.

"It looks like they are intercepting them," Jen Janicek, one of his daughters, concluded. She was a lovely young girl with light skin, green eyes and blonde hair. She was wearing a grey sweater with dark slacks and slippers. Her hair was pulled back in a ponytail as she had planned on going out to say good bye to all of her friends before the Red Javelin arrived. She was going to the Moscow Academy starting that next August to study to become a pilot, just like her father. But the weapons that were coming to Earth were going to destroy the dreams and hopes of billions.

"I'll be damned," President Janicek said softly. "They must be survivors of the Second Fleet."

The Janicek family and the rest of the eight solar systems began to make the same observation.

Even Andrew Brey O'Connell noticed the seven ships on his screens while he watched from his massive compound. He screamed at the monitors as he realized what the seven ships were about to do. O'Connell picked up a swivel chair and threw it across the room in a rage. He and his staff had not thought about giving the Red Javelin weapons armed escorts. He cursed at himself for that oversight. He realized that if the weapons were detonated in space that their power and range would be unpredictable. He told some of his staff to warn the Glorious Leader to take cover underground, just in case.

The Yutong brothers and Azeem Nour looked at O'Connell with concern when he advised them of the same. Nour scooped up the limp Siobhan Collins and they raced for the elevator that would take them all several hundred feet under the planet surface.

"Fire!" Jayne Starr screamed.

She let loose a dozen bursts of lasers before she cut her ship to the left to race for the largest sun. Marco and Benson followed suit. Marco also fired his last rocket.

Renee Starr fired her lasers at her target. She did not know why, but she was crying as she fired. Perhaps it was the knowledge that her life was about to end. She had one last thing to say as she turned her steering column hard left. "Sis! I love you so much!"

Soto and Shea fired as did Tulley. All seven ships were racing against the inevitable. Marco screamed out loud for each of them to head straight for the sun and cut right at the last possible moment.

Their speeds increased dramatically due to the gravitational force of the sun. Marco could hear his computer warning him as his craft was flying over nine hundred thousand kilometers an hour and climbing. He struggled with his steering column and gritted his teeth as he prepared for the blast to catch him.

Then the world took in a collective sigh of relief.

The largest explosion in the history of mankind ignited there in deep space as the eight Red Javelin weapons exploded simultaneously. Jayne's hopes for a chain reaction became a reality as the other three weapons exploded when the deadly energy from the other eight enveloped them. The darkness of space lit up as if a super nova had occurred from out of nowhere. The viewers of the eight solar systems had to cover their eyes from the brightness of the event. The white lights from the eruption spread for several astronomical units and anything in the surrounding solar system began to lose power as the light passed through it.

Two Raumschiffs from the First Fleet had been sent into the area and were caught in the blast. The metal of the two ships began to melt when the white energy of the Red Javelin explosions enveloped them. Each ship had a crew of fifty on board. They all died as their flesh began to boil. The Raumschiff they were in melted around them as they let out blood curdling screams of agony.

White and Dell had made it to the other side of the sun just before the explosions. They lost all power on their small fighter ships as well. Dell wept with guilt in that she had not stayed and helped the others. For what little time she had left in her life, running from her moment of truth would be her greatest regret.

White cursed and slammed her hands onto her control panel. She had to get back to her family one way or another. She found that her on board computer was not operating as the bright white energy swirled by her. She heard a sound of sizzling around her and noticed that the metal on the hull of her small fighter ship was bright red and white from the intense heat. Her ship was melting before her eyes. White screamed in panic as she watched the metal on her space craft begin to drip away into liquid. The intense heat began to sear through her enviro-suit. The agony of her flesh beginning to fall in clumps from her body was too much for her to bear. She screamed as she passed out. Her death followed soon thereafter.

Dell met a similar fate. As she felt herself burning she pulled out her laser pistol and aimed it at her head. She was screaming in pain as the weapons energy was eating through her ship's hull and her enviro-suit. To end the agony she felt from her flesh burning off her body, she pulled the trigger of her laser and blew the top of her own head off. The three space stations that were orbiting Sikorsky's Planet lost all power from the radioactive and electrical charges of the blast. The entire planet below lost all power as well. The Glorious Leader saw all of his screens go blank and his lights dim and flicker during the explosion. Admiral Perdicas cursed when the entire First Fleet lost all of their power as well.

On board the *Waterloo*, the entire crew cursed and cried out as their ship went pitch black. Only Dirk Fenster smiled at the power loss. He immediately picked up one of the metal chairs and using one of the legs of that chair, began to try and force the sliding door of the prison cell open.

Andrew Brey O'Connell cursed out loud as his massive weapons facility began to shut down. He was glad that he and his most trusted advisors and guards had gotten underground before the power of the weapon reached the planet surface. He wondered how many would be dead by this time tomorrow. In a sofa nearby, Siobhan Collins smiled. She was still unable to move due to the stun dart that had been injected into her. But she could smile. Billions had been saved. And when the effects of the stun dart wore off she intended to kill the man she loved.

As for the seven brave pilots that had the audacity to stand up and take the risk, they tried to outrun the wave of white light. Benson began to scream out about the colors surrounding her. It was a kaleidoscope of brilliant colors that she had never seen in her life. It was beautiful and seemed somehow soothing to her. She knew that death was coming for her soon, but the patterns of the lights gave her a feeling that everything was okay. It was a fine way to die.

"I see it!" Marco responded to her as he observed the same phenomenon. "Pinks! Yellows! Reds! I have never seen so many colors! What is it from?"

The Starr sisters, Soto, Talley and Shea made similar comments.

For a brief second Marco thought he saw the outline of a woman before him. She was multi-colored like the lights that surrounded his ship. Her hair was blown as if by an unseen wind as she opened her arms to Marco, seemingly to embrace him. The outline of her features were beautiful. He thought he saw her smile. He had seen her before, sometimes in his dreams. He heard her voice, which was the same voice he had heard on the Blood Moon.

"It is time."

And then everything went black for the seven brave souls that willingly sacrificed themselves so that billions of others might live.

They were each at peace.

EPILOGUE

Nadia Janicek was only twelve years old. She was sitting on the rug in the main room with her family watching the battle as it unfolded. When the eleven Red Javelin's exploded she gasped. "Grandfather!"

"Yes my dear?" Janos Janicek responded to her.

"There was a woman that talked to me in my dreams," Nadia stood up and pointed to the massive explosion on their three dimensional view screen.

The retired Admiral felt a chill rise up in his spine as he recalled his numerous nightmares that had been recurring almost nightly. "A woman in your dreams? What did she say?"

"The fire in the sky grandfather!" Nadia pointed at the explosion. "She said there would be a fire in the sky. She said it was a sign that we had to come together and fight."

Janos Janicek stood up from his comfortable chair and felt as if destiny was calling him. He had put the dreams of Melita Gorski out of his mind. He wrote it off as his guilty conscience playing tricks with his subconscious mind. But his granddaughter had been visited in her dreams as well. Janicek felt as if the temperature in the room was dropping. He looked around the wall of his massive meeting area in the presidential castle. On the stone walls were plaques for his seven Medals of Valor, six Medals of Honor, and three Medals for Meritorious Service, two Security Council awards for Captain of the Year and three for Admiral of the Year. He pursed his lips as his wives, children and grandchildren watched the three dimensional view of the massive explosion. He felt for the seven pilots that had sacrificed themselves to save life. He felt a lump grow in his throat as he knew that Captain Allen and Admiral Khan would have been proud to have had seven brave souls such as those men and women on their crew.

And while they were fighting for justice, he was sitting on his butt drinking wine.

"Grandfather, what are you doing?" Little Janos Janicek, III, asked as he saw him stand.

"I know I promised all of you that I was retired. I must break that promise," Janicek told his family. He shook his head, smiled and then turned to his oldest wife, Elianna. "Honey, in the main closet downstairs are my old uniforms. Please get them for me."

"What are you doing, Janos?" Elianna looked at him with concern.

"There are hundreds of my friends living in retirement. I am going to find them. Then I am going to get myself to all of the floating museums near the space station, the moon and Mars so I can get on board the eight retired Battle Cruisers that are located there. Once I do that I will see if they are all still operational."

"Why grandfather?" Janos, III asked.

"Because I have one last war to fight," Janos Janicek told his family with conviction as he left the room.

TO BE CONTINUED IN RED JAVELIN
SAGA BOOK 4